S0-ABV-925

Karen Hesse

Out of the Dust

Annotations by
Mechthild Hesse

Ernst Klett Verlag
Stuttgart Düsseldorf Leipzig

This edition of *Out of the Dust* contains the complete and unabridged text of the original. American spelling conventions have been preserved and are also used in the annotations.

Annotations by Mechthild Hesse, Bad Homburg.

Gedruckt auf Papier aus chlorfrei gebleichtem Zellstoff, säurefrei

1. Auflage   A 1 5 4 3 2 1 | 2006 05 04 03 02

Alle Drucke dieser Auflage können im Unterricht nebeneinander benutzt werden. Die letzte Zahl bezeichnet das Jahr dieses Druckes.
Copyright © 1997 by Karen Hesse. All rights reserved.
Published by arrangement with Scholastic Inc.
Dieses Werk wurde vermittelt durch die Literarische Agentur Thomas Schlück GmbH, 30827 Garbsen.
© für diese Ausgabe : Ernst Klett Verlag GmbH, Stuttgart 2002.
Alle Rechte vorbehalten.
Internetadresse: www.klett-verlag.de

Redaktion: Dr. Hartmut K. Selke

Cover photo by Dorothea Lange: Corbis/Picture Press
Foto der Autorin S. 3: Cheril Liston © 1992
Repro: Reprotechnik Ruit
Druck: Gutmann+Co. GmbH, Talheim
Printed in Germany.
ISBN 3-12-578180-9

Contents

Biographical Note   5
Language   6

Out of the Dust

Winter 1934   7
Spring 1934 30
Summer 1934 41
Autumn 1934 63
Winter 1935 69
Spring 1935 103
Summer 1935 128
Autumn 1935 138

Supplementary Texts

1. Mean Clouds 152
2. Mother Road – Route 66 154
3. Map of Oklahoma and Northern Texas 155
4. Dusty Old Dust (Woody Guthrie) 156
5. An Excerpt from *The Grapes of Wrath* by John Steinbeck   158

To Benda Bowen,
who is much more
than an editor

I extend heartfelt thanks to Eileen Christelow,
Kate, Rachel and Randy Hesse,
Liza Ketchum, Jeffrey and Bernice Millman,
Maryann Sparks,
and the Oklahoma Historical Society.

Biographical Note

Karen Hesse was born in Baltimore, Maryland, in 1952. She writes about herself:

"While growing up in Baltimore I dreamed of becoming many things: an archaeologist, an ambassador, an actor, an author. In 1969, I attended Towson State College as a theater major, but transferred after two semesters to the University of Maryland, where I eventually earned a B.A. in English [...].

"From the time I was ten I thought of myself as 'good with words,' thanks to a perceptive and supportive fifth grade teacher. Mrs. Datnoff believed I could be a professional writer some day and because she believed, I believed too. Though I gave up all my other career dreams, I never gave up dreaming of publication. It took more than thirty years to see that fifth-grade dream come true. I don't know whether that makes me extremely patient or just plain stubborn.

"I have earned wages as a waitress, a nanny, a librarian, a personnel officer, an agricultural laborer, an advertising secretary, a typesetter, a proofreader, a mental-health-care provider, a substitute teacher, and a book reviewer. In and around the edges of all those jobs I have written poems, stories, and books, books, books. [...]

"I love writing. I can't wait to get to my keyboard every morning. I also love reading, hiking, spending time with friends and family, traveling, and music – both playing it and listening to it.

"Young readers are the most challenging, demanding, and rewarding of audiences. Adults often ask why I write for the younger set. My reply: I can't think of anyone I'd rather write for."

Karen Hesse lives in Vermont with her husband and two daughters. *Out of the Dust* was awarded the Newbery Medal for 1998.

Language

The language Karen Hesse uses in *Out of the Dust* is that of an Oklahoma farm girl. It is characterized by a number of non-standard expressions. For example "a ways south of here" (**8** 24) means "a certain distance south of here." Non-standard expressions are explained in the vocabulary notes and the fact that they are non-standard is pointed out. We recommend that you do not use these expressions yourself.

We have annotated *Out of the Dust* quite generously, still there might be a few words that you are not yet familiar with. Before you take your dictionary from the shelf, we would like you to try if one of the following techniques might help you to understand the unknown word.

1. Word family
Try to remember how words are put together in English. If you know the word "bright" (**35** 21), you will easily deduce that "to brighten" means "to make bright."

2. Similar words in other languages that you already know
This includes German words that are similar to English words. An example is "dunes" (**48** 2). Looking over the countryside covered with sand, the narrator sees nothing but "dunes of rippled dust."

3. Context
Examining the context in which a word appears is the best way of finding out the meaning of difficult words. By looking carefully at the words or sentences before and after an unknown word or expression, you can often discover its meaning. An example is "erupt" (**58** 2). When you look at the context you will find out that the verb describes a volcano that suddenly becomes active.

4. Sound
Sometimes, though rarely, saying a word out loud may show you its meaning. "Ponging" (**72** 20) in the chapter "First Rain" is such a case. When you say the word aloud, you can almost hear the raindrops beating on the roof.

Finally, it is important to accept that you will not understand every word when reading in a foreign language or even in your own language. Do not let this frustrate you. You need not know every word to understand the general sense of a sentence or paragraph.

Beginning: August 1920

As summer wheat came ripe,
so did I,
born at home, on the kitchen floor.
Ma crouched,
barefoot, bare bottomed
over the swept boards,
because that's where Daddy said it'd be best.

I came too fast for the doctor,
10 bawling as soon as Daddy wiped his hand around
inside my mouth.
To hear Ma tell it,
I hollered myself red the day I was born.
Red's the color I've stayed ever since.

15 Daddy named me Billie Jo.
He wanted a boy.
Instead,
he got a long-legged girl
with a wide mouth
20 and cheekbones like bicycle handles.
He got a redheaded, freckle-faced, narrow-hipped girl
with a fondness for apples
and a hunger for playing fierce piano.

From the earliest I can remember
25 I've been restless in this

---

2 **wheat** a type of grain *(Weizen)* – 5 **to crouch** to sit on one's heels – 6 **bare bottomed** having no underpants on – 7 **to sweep** (swept, swept) to clean (with a broom) – **board** piece of wood *(Brett)* – 10 **to bawl** to cry loud – 13 **to holler** to cry loud – 21 **freckles** *Sommersprossen* – **narrow-hipped** figure with narrow hips *(= Hüften)* – 22 **fondness for** love of, liking for – 23 **fierce** strong, wild

little Panhandle shack we call home,
always getting in Ma's way with my
pointy elbows, my fidgety legs.
By the summer I turned nine Daddy had
5   given up about having a boy.
He tried making me do.
I look just like him,
I can handle myself most everywhere he puts me,
even on the tractor,
10   though I don't like that much.

Ma tried having other babies.
It never seemed to go right, except with me.
But this morning
Ma let on as how she's expecting again.
15   Other than the three of us
there's not much family to speak of.
Daddy, the only boy Kelby left
since Grandpa died
from a cancer
20   that ate up the most of his skin,
and Aunt Ellis,
almost fourteen years older than Daddy
and living in Lubbock,
a ways south of here,
25   and a whole world apart
to hear Daddy tell it.
And Ma, with only Great-uncle Floyd,
old as ancient Indian bones,

---

1 **Panhandle** Oklahoma Panhandle (see map p. 155) – **shack** hut, cabin –
3 **pointy** pointed *(spitz)* – **fidgety** always moving, nervous – 6 **to make s.o. do**
here: to be satisfied with s.o. as a substitute – 14 **to let on** to say, to express – **as**
how *here:* that – **to be expecting** to expect a baby, to be pregnant – 19 **cancer**
serious illness *(Krebs)* – 23 **Lubbock** town in Texas (cf. map p. 155) – **a ways** a
long way – 28 **ancient** ['eɪnʃənt] very old

and mean as a rattler,
rotting away in that room down in Dallas.

I'll be nearly fourteen
just like Aunt Ellis was when Daddy was born
by the time this baby comes.

Wonder if Daddy'll get his boy this time?

January 1934

Rabbit Battles

Mr. Noble and
Mr. Romney have a bet going
as to who can kill the most rabbits.
It all started at the rabbit drive last Monday
over to Sturgis
when Mr. Noble got himself worked up
about the damage done to his crop by jacks.
Mr. Romney swore he'd had more rabbit trouble
than anyone in Cimarron County.
They pledged revenge on the rabbit population;
wagering who could kill more.

They ought to just shut up.
Betting on how many rabbits they can kill.
Honestly!
Grown men clubbing bunnies to death.
Makes me sick to my stomach.

---

1 mean bad, vicious *(bösartig)* – **rattler** rattlesnake *(Klapperschlange)* –
6 **wonder** I wonder – 10 **to have a bet going** *here:* to have a competition
(= Wettkampf) – 11 **as to** concerning *(was anbetrifft)* – 14 **to get o.s. worked
up about** to get excited, nervous about – 15 **to do damage** to harm *(schaden)* –
crop plants a farmer grows on his fields – **jack** jackrabbit – 16 **to swear** (swore,
sworn) *schwören* – 17 **Cimarron County** district in northern Oklahoma (see
map p. 155) – 18 **to pledge** to swear, to promise – **revenge** *Rache* – 19 **to wager**
to bet – 23 **to club** to beat – **bunny** rabbit

I know rabbits eat what they shouldn't,
especially this time of year when they could hop
halfway to Liberal
and still not find food,
5 but Miss Freeland says
if we keep
plowing under the stuff they ought to be eating,
what are they supposed to do?

Mr. Noble and
10 Mr. Romney came home from Sturgis Monday
with twenty rabbits apiece. A tie.
It should've stopped there. But
Mr. Romney wasn't satisfied.
He said,
15 "Noble cheated.
He brought in rabbits somebody else killed."
And so the contest goes on.

Those men,
they used to be best friends.
20 Now they can't be civil with each other.
They scowl as they pass on the street.
I'm scowling too,
but scowling won't bring the rabbits back.
They're all skinned and cooked and eaten by now.
25 At least they didn't end up in
Romney and Noble's cook pots.
They went to families
that needed the meat.

January 1934

---

2 **hop** jump – 3 **Liberal** city in Kansas, just north of the Oklahoma border – 7 **to plow** (BE to plough) *pflügen* – 11 **apiece** each – **tie** *Unentschieden* – 15 **to cheat** to be dishonest – 17 **contest** ['kɒntest] competition *(Wettkampf)* – 20 **civil** polite, well-behaved – 21 **to scowl** to make a face that shows one's anger

Losing Livie

Livie Killian moved away.
I didn't want her to go.
We'd been friends since first grade.

The farewell party was
Thursday night
at the Old Rock Schoolhouse.

Livie
had something to tease each of us about,
like Ray
sleeping through reading class,
and Hillary,
who on her speed-writing test put
an "even ton" of children
instead of an "even ten."

Livie said good-bye to each of us,
separately.
She gave me a picture she'd made of me sitting
in front of a piano,
wearing my straw hat,
an apple halfway to my mouth.

I handed Livie the memory book we'd all
filled with our different slants.
I couldn't get the muscles in my throat relaxed enough
to tell her how much I'd miss her.

Livie
helped clean up her own party,
wiping spilled lemonade,

---

9 **to tease s.o.** to make fun of s.o. – 14 **even** an even number can be divided by two *(gerade)* – 23 **slant** line that is neither horizontal nor vertical; *here:* handwriting – 24 **muscles** ['mʌslz] – **throat** the upper part of the passage from the mouth to the stomach – 28 **to spill** to flow from an overturned glass, etc.

gathering sandwich crusts,
sweeping cookie crumbs from the floor,
while the rest of us went home
to study for semester reviews.

5 Now Livie's gone west,
out of the dust,
on her way to California,
where the wind takes a rest sometimes.
And I'm wondering what kind of friend I am,
10 wanting my feet on that road to another place,
instead of Livie's.

January 1934

Me and Mad Dog

Arley Wanderdale,
15 who teaches music once a week at our school,
though Ma says he's no teacher at all,
just a local song plugger,
Arley Wanderdale asked
if I'd like to play a piano solo
20 at the Palace Theatre on Wednesday night.

I grinned,
pleased to be asked, and said,
"That'd be all right."

I didn't know if Ma would let me.
25 She's an old mule on the subject of my schooling.
She says,
"You stay home on weeknights, Billie Jo."
And mostly that's what I do.

---

1 **to gather** to collect – 2 **crumbs** [krʌmz] small bits of s.th. *(Krumen)* – 4 **review** *here:* test – **17 plugger** music lover – 25 **mule** *Maultier; here:* a stubborn (= *störrisch*) person

But Arley Wanderdale said,
"The management asked me to
bring them talent, Billie Jo,
and I thought of you."

Even before Mad Dog Craddock? I wondered.

"You and Mad Dog," Arley Wanderdale said.

Darn that blue-eyed boy
with his fine face and his
smooth voice,
twice as good
as a plowboy has any right to be.
I suspected Mad Dog had come first
to Arley Wanderdale's mind,
but I didn't get too riled.
Not so riled I couldn't say yes.

January 1934

Permission to Play

Sometimes,
when Ma is busy in the kitchen,
or scrubbing,
or doing wash,
I can ask her something in such a way
I annoy her just enough to get an answer,
but not so much I get a no.

That's a way I've found of gaining what I want,
by catching Ma off guard,
especially when I'm after permission to play piano.

---

7 **darn** *(informal)* damn – **9 smooth** [smuːð] soft – 12 **to suspect** to assume, to think – 14 **riled** *(informal)* angry – 20 **to scrub** to rub hard, to clean using a stiff brush – 23 **to annoy s.o.** to make s.o. angry – 25 **to gain** to win; *here:* to get – 26 **off guard** not paying attention

Right out asking her is no good.
She always gets testy about me playing,
even though she's the one who truly taught me.

Anyway, this time I caught her in the
5   slow stirring of biscuits,
her mind on other things,
maybe the baby growing inside her, I don't know,
but anyhow,
she was distracted enough,
10 I was determined enough,
this time I got just what I wanted.
Permission to play at the Palace.

January 1934

On Stage

15 When I point my fingers at the keys,
             the music
springs straight out of me.
             Right hand
playing notes sharp as
20   tongues,
telling stories while the
           smooth
buttery rhythms back me up
           on the left.

25 Folks sway in the
           Palace aisles

---

2 **testy** bad-tempered, easily made angry – 5 **to stir biscuits** ['bɪskɪts] to make the dough *(= Teig)* for biscuits – 9 **distracted** not paying attention *(abgelenkt)* – 10 **to be determined** to have made a clear decision *(entschlossen sein)* – 15 **key** [kiː] part of a piano or a keyboard that is pressed down with one's fingers – 25 **to sway** to move one's body back and forth – 26 **aisle** [aɪl] long narrow passage separating rows of seats in a church or theater

grinning and stomping and
                    out of breath,
and the rest, eyes shining,
                    fingers snapping,
feet tapping. It's the best
                    I've ever felt,
playing hot piano,
                    sizzling with
Mad Dog,
                    swinging with the Black Mesa Boys,
or on my own,
                    crazy,
pestering the keys.
                    That is
heaven.
                    How supremely
heaven
                    playing piano
can be.

January 1934

Birthday for F.D.R.

I played so well
on Wednesday night,
Arley put his arm across my shoulder
and asked me to come and
perform at the President's birthday ball.
Ma can't say no to this one.
It's for President Roosevelt.

---

1 **to stomp** to beat the rhythm with one's feet – 8 **to sizzle** to make a hissing
sound (i.e. like steaks being fried) – 13 **to pester** to annoy by doing s.th. again
and again – **to pester the keys** *(informal)* to keep playing – 16 **supremely**
[su:ˈpri:mlɪ] gloriously – 21 **F.D.R.** Franklin Delano Roosevelt [ˈrəʊzəvelt] 1882
– 1945, U.S. President 1933 – 1945

Not that Mr. Roosevelt will actually be there,
but the money collected at the ball,
along with balls all over the country,
will go,
5 in the President's name,
to the Warm Springs Foundation,
where Mr. Roosevelt stayed once when he was sick.

Someday,
I plan to play for President Franklin Delano Roosevelt
10 himself.
Maybe I'll go all the way to the White House in
Washington, D.C.
In the meantime,
it's pretty nice
15 Arley asking me to play twice,
for Joyce City.

January 1934

Not Too Much To Ask

We haven't had a good crop in three years,
20 not since the bounty of '31,
and we're all whittled down to the bone these days,
even Ma, with her new round belly,
but still
when the committee came asking,
25 Ma donated:

---

6 **Warm Springs** health resort *(= Badeort)* in Georgia that Franklin D. Roosevelt
visited in 1924 after an attack of polio *(= Kinderlähmung)*; Roosevelt
established the W.S. Foundation in 1927 – **foundation** *Stiftung* – 16 **Joyce City**
does not exist, invented by the author – 19 **crop** farm produce grown and
gathered in one season *(Ernte)* – 20 **bounty** very good harvest, riches – 21 **to be
whittled down to the bone** to be very, very thin (**to whittle** = *schnitzen*) – 25 **to
donate** ['dəʊneɪt] to give away for a good cause *(spenden)*

three jars of apple sauce
and
some cured pork,
and a
feed-sack nightie she'd sewn for our coming baby.

February 1934

Mr. Hardly's Money Handling

It was Daddy's birthday
and Ma decided to bake him a cake.
There wasn't
money enough for anything like a real present.
Ma sent me to fetch the extras
with fifty cents she'd been hiding away.
"Don't go to Joyce City, Billie," she said.
"You can get what we need down Hardly's store."

I slipped the coins into my sweater pocket, the pocket
without the hole,
thinking about how many sheets of new music
fifty cents would buy.

Mr. Hardly glared
when the Wonder Bread door
banged shut behind me.
He squinted as I creaked across the wooden floor.

---

1 **jar** container made of glass – **apple sauce** *Apfelmus* – 3 **cured** preserved,
smoked – 5 **feed-sack nightie** baby pyjama made from a feed sack (a sack tied to
a horse's mouth and that the horse eats from) – 18 **sheets of music** *Noten* – 20 **to
glare** to look with an angry expression on one's face – 21 **Wonder Bread** a brand
name (there was an advertisement for Wonder Bread on the door of the shop) –
22 **to bang shut** to close with a loud noise – 23 **to squint** to look with one's eyes
partly closed – **to creak** to make an unpleasant noise, i.e. when a wooden door
that is not well-oiled is opened

Mr. Hardly was in the habit
of charging too much for his stale food,
and he made bad change when he thought
he could get away with it.
I squinted back at him as I gave him Ma's order.

5

Mr. Hardly's
been worse than normal
since his attic filled with dust
and collapsed under the weight.
10 He hired folks for the repairs,
and argued over every nail and every
little minute.
The whole place took
shoveling for days before he could
15 open again and
some stock was so bad it
had to be thrown away.

The stove clanked in the corner
as Mr. Hardly filled Ma's order.
20 I could smell apples,
ground coffee, and peppermint.
I sorted through the patterns on the feed bags,
sneezed dust,
blew my nose.

25 When Mr. Hardly finished sacking my things,
I paid the bill,

---

1 **to be in the habit of** to usually do s.th. – 2 **to charge too much** to ask too much money – **stale** old and dry – 3 **to make bad change** to return an incorrect sum of money to a customer *(falsch herausgeben)* – 8 **attic** floor under the roof – 10 **to hire s.o.** to give work to s.o., to employ s.o. – 13 **the place took shoveling** it was necessary to shovel the dust out of the place – 16 **stock** *here:* food, goods – 18 **to clank** to make a metallic noise – 21 **ground** *gemahlen* – 23 **to sneeze** *niesen* – 24 **to blow one's nose** to wipe one's nose with a handkerchief

and tucking the list in my pocket along with the change,
hurried home,
so Ma could bake the cake before Daddy came in.

But after Ma emptied the sack,
setting each packet out on the
oilcloth, she counted her change
and I remembered with a sinking feeling
that I hadn't kept an eye on
Mr. Hardly's money handling,
and Mr. Hardly had cheated again.
Only this time he'd cheated himself, giving us
four cents extra.

So while Ma mixed a cake,
I walked back to Mr. Hardly's store,
back through the dust,
back through the Wonder Bread door,
and thinking about the secondhand music
in a moldy box at the shop in Joyce City,
music I could have for two cents a sheet,
I placed Mr. Hardly's overpayment on the counter
and turned to head back home.

Mr. Hardly cleared his throat and
I wondered for a moment
if he'd call me back to offer a piece of peppermint
or pick me out an apple from the crate,
but he didn't,
and that's okay.
Ma would have thrown a fit
if I'd taken a gift from him.

February 1934

---

1 **to tuck** to put – 6 **oilcloth** plastic tablecloth – 18 **moldy** *schimmelig* – 25 **crate**
box – 28 **to throw a fit** to get extremely angry

Fifty Miles South of Home

In Amarillo,
wind
blew plate-glass windows in,
5   tore electric signs down,
ripped wheat
straight out of the ground.

February 1934

Rules of Dining

10 Ma has rules for setting the table.
I place plates upside down,
glasses bottom side up,
napkins folded over forks, knives, and spoons.

When dinner is ready,
15 we sit down together
and Ma says,
"Now."

We shake out our napkins,
spread them on our laps,
20 and flip over our glasses and plates,
exposing neat circles,
round comments
on what life would be without dust.

Daddy says,
25 "The potatoes are peppered plenty tonight, Polly,"

---

2 **Amarillo** city in northern Texas (see map p. 155) – 4 **plate-glass** made of very thick glass – 5 **to tear down** (tore, torn) *herunterreißen* – 6 **to rip** to tear – 9 **rule** regulation – 13 **napkin** piece of paper or cloth used to protect one's clothes and to wipe one's mouth while eating – 19 **lap** part of the lower body *(Schoß)* – 21 **to expose** to show, to make visible – 22 **comment** statement of opinion

and
"Chocolate milk for dinner, aren't we in clover!"
when really all our pepper and chocolate,
it's nothing but dust.

I heard word from Livie Killian.
The Killians can't find work,
can't get food.
Livie's brother, Reuben, fifteen last summer,
took off, thinking to make it on his own.
I hope he's okay.

With a baby growing inside Ma,
it scares me thinking, Where would we be without
somewhere to live?
Without some work to do?
Without something to eat?
At least we've got milk. Even if we have to chew it.

February 1934

Breaking Drought

After seventy days
of wind and sun,
of wind and clouds,
of wind and sand,
after seventy days,
of wind and dust,
a little
rain
came.

February 1934

---

2 **to be in clover** to live a rich, luxurious life (**clover** = *Klee*) – 12 **to scare s.o.**
to frighten s.o. – 16 **to chew** to bite food with one's teeth – 18 **drought** [draʊt]
period without rain

21

Dazzled

In the kitchen she is my ma,
in the barn and the fields she is my daddy's wife,
but in the parlor Ma is something different.
5   She isn't much to look at,
so long and skinny,
her teeth poor,
her dark hair always needing a wash, but
from the time I was four,
10 I remember being dazzled by her
whenever she played the piano.

Daddy bought it, an old Cramer,
his wedding gift to her.
She came to this house and found gaps in the walls,
15 a rusty bed, no running water,
and that piano,
gleaming in the corner.

Daddy gets soft eyes, standing behind her while she plays.
I want someone to look that way at me.

20 On my fifth birthday,
Ma sat me down beside her
and started me to reading music,
started me to playing.
I'm not half so good as Ma.
25 She can pull Daddy into the parlor
even after the last milking, when he's so beat
he barely knows his own name
and all he wants
is a mattress under his bones.

---

1 **dazzled** *here:* overwhelmed, deeply impressed – 3 **barn** building in which
animals and hay, etc., are kept – 4 **parlor** sitting room – 6 **skinny** very thin –
12 **Cramer** piano brand name – 14 **gap** hole – 17 **to gleam** to shine softly –
26 **beat** extremely tired – 27 **barely** hardly

You've got to be something
to get his notice that time of day,
but Ma can.
I'm not half so good with my crazy playing
as she is with her fine tunes and her
fancy fingerwork.
But I'm good enough for Arley, I guess.

March 1934

Debts

Daddy is thinking
of taking a loan from Mr. Roosevelt and his men,
to get some new wheat planted
where the winter crop has spindled out and died.
Mr. Roosevelt promises
Daddy won't have to pay a dime
till the crop comes in.

Daddy says,
"I can turn the fields over,
start again.
It's sure to rain soon.
Wheat's sure to grow."

Ma says, "What if it doesn't?"

Daddy takes off his hat,
roughs up his hair,
puts the hat back on.
"Course it'll rain," he says.

_____

2 **notice** *here:* attention – 6 **fancy** very good, outstanding – 9 **debt** [det] money
one owes *(Schulden)* – 11 **to take a loan** to borrow money – 13 **to spindle out**
to become very thin – 15 **dime** 10-cent coin; the amount of 10 cents, i.e. a small
sum of money

Ma says, "Bay,
it hasn't rained enough to grow wheat in
three years."

Daddy looks like a fight brewing.
5   He takes that red face of his out to the barn,
to keep from feuding with my pregnant ma.

I ask Ma
how,
after all this time,
10 Daddy still believes in rain.

"Well, it rains enough," Ma says,
"now and again,
to keep a person hoping.
But even if it didn't
15 your daddy would have to believe.
It's coming on spring,
and he's a farmer."

March 1934

Foul as Maggoty Stew

20 Arley Wanderdale said
the rehearsals for *Sunny of Sunnyside*
shouldn't take me out of school
more than twice next week.

When I told Ma she got angry about
25 my missing school to play piano for some show.

---

1 **Bay** short for Bayard, the father's first name – 4 **like a fight brewing** as if he
was going to fight – 6 **to feud** [fju:d] to fight – 16 **it's coming on spring** *(non-
standard)* spring is coming – 19 **maggoty** ['mægətɪ] full of worms – **stew** soup –
21 **rehearsal** [rɪ'hɜ:sl] practice performance of a play

Me and Daddy,
we're trying our best to please Ma,
for fear of what it might do to the baby if we don't.
I don't know why she's
so against my playing.
She says that school is important,
but I do all right in school.
I know she doesn't like the kind
of music I play,
but sometimes I think she's
just plain jealous
when I'm at the piano
and she's not.
And maybe she's a little afraid
of me going somewhere with the music
she can't follow.
Or of the music taking me
so far away one day
I'll never come home.
Whatever the reason, she said I couldn't do it.
Arley had to get somebody to take my place.

I do as she says. I go to school,
and in the afternoons I come home,
run through my chores,
do my reading and my math work at the
kitchen table
and all the while I glare at Ma's back with a scowl
foul as maggoty stew.

March 1934

---

11 **plain** simply – **jealous** ['dʒeləs] wanting s.th. that s.o. else has – 24 **to run through chores** [tʃɔːz] to do jobs in the household – 27 **all the while** while doing this

State Tests

When I got home I told Ma
our school scored higher than the
whole state on achievement tests and
5 I scored top of eighth grade.

Ma nodded.
"I knew you could."

That's all she said.

She was proud,
10 I could tell.
But she didn't
coo like Mad Dog's ma. Or
go on
like Mrs. Killian used to do.
15 Daddy says,
"That's not your ma's way."
But I wish it was.
I wish she'd give me a little more to hold on to than
"I knew you could."
20 Instead she makes me feel like she's just
taking me in like I was
so much flannel dry on the line.

March 1934

Fields of Flashing Light

25 I heard the wind rise,
and stumbled from my bed,

---

3 **to score higher** to have better results – 4 **achievement test** standardized test
taken at the end of the school year – 5 **to score top** to be best – 12 **to coo** to make
soft loving noises – 22 **flannel** piece of cloth – 26 **to stumble** to walk unsteadily

down the stairs,
out the front door,
into the yard.
The night sky kept flashing,
lightning danced down on its spindly legs.

I sensed it before I knew it was coming.
I heard it,
smelled it,
tasted it.

Dust.

While Ma and Daddy slept,
the dust came,
tearing up fields where the winter wheat,
set for harvest in June,
stood helpless.
I watched the plants,
surviving after so much drought and so much wind,
I watched them fry,
or
flatten,
or blow away,
like bits of cast-off rags.

It wasn't until the dust turned toward the house,
like a fired locomotive,
and I fled,
barefoot and breathless, back inside,
it wasn't until the dust
hissed against the windows,
until it ratcheted the roof,
that Daddy woke.

---

5 **lightning** sudden flashing light *(Blitz)* – **spindly** very thin – 6 **to sense** to feel –
22 **to cast off** to throw away – **rags** old clothes – 25 **to flee** (fled, fled) to run
away – 28 **to hiss** to make a sharp sound – 29 **to ratchet s.th.** *here:* to make s.th.
rattle, to shake

He ran into the storm,
his overalls half-hooked over his union suit.
"Daddy!" I called. "You can't stop dust."

Ma told me to
5   cover the beds,
push the scatter rugs against the doors,
dampen the rags around the windows.
Wiping dust out of everything,
she made coffee and biscuits,
10 waiting for Daddy to come in.

Sometime after four,
rubbing low on her back,
Ma sank down into a chair at the kitchen table
and covered her face.
15 Daddy didn't come back for hours,
not
until the temperature dropped so low,
it brought snow.

Ma and I sighed, grateful,
20 staring out at the dirty flakes,
but our relief didn't last.
The wind snatched that snow right off the fields,
leaving behind a sea of dust,
waves and
25 waves and
waves of
dust,
rippling across our yard.

---

2 **union suit** ['juːnɪən suːt] underwear (underpants and undershirt combined) –
6 **scatter rug** small carpet covering part of the floor *(Läufer)* – 7 **to dampen** to
make wet – 12 **to rub** to massage – 19 **grateful** thankful – 21 **relief** feeling of
happiness after s.th. bad or unpleasant is over *(Erleichterung)* – 22 **to snatch
off** to take away quickly – 28 **to ripple** to move like a wave

Daddy came in,
he sat across from Ma and blew his nose.
Mud streamed out.
He coughed and spit out
mud.
If he had cried,
his tears would have been mud too,
but he didn't cry.
And neither did Ma.

March 1934

---

3 **mud** wet dust *(Schlamm)* – 4 **to cough** [kɒf] *husten*

Tested by Dust

While we sat
taking our six-weeks test,
the wind rose
5   and the sand blew
right through the cracks in the schoolhouse wall,
right through the gaps around the window glass,
and by the time the tests were done,
each and every one of us
10 was coughing pretty good and we all
needed a bath.

I hope we get bonus points
for testing in a dust storm.

April 1934

15 **Banks**

Ma says,
everything we lost
when the banks closed
'cause they didn't have enough cash to go around,
20 all the money that's ours
is coming back to us in full.

Good.

Now we have money for a doctor
when the baby comes.

April 1934

---

6 **crack** opening – 12 **bonus points** extra points – 19 **'cause** because

Beat Wheat

County Agent Dewey
had some pretty bad news.
One quarter of the wheat is lost:
blown away or withered up.
What remains is little more than
a wisp of what it should be.
And every day we have no rain,
more wheat dies.

County Agent Dewey says, "Soon
there won't be enough wheat
for seed to plant next fall."

The piano is some comfort in all this.
I go to it and I forget the dust for hours,
testing my long fingers on wild rhythms,
but Ma slams around in the kitchen when I play
and after a while she sends me to the store.
Joe De La Flor doesn't see me pass him by;
he rides his fences, dazed by dust.
I wince at the sight of his rib-thin cattle.
But he's not even seeing them.
I look at Joe and know our future is drying up
and blowing away with the dust.

April 1934

---

1 **beat** beaten down, destroyed – 2 **County Agent** government employee who
advises farmers – 5 **to wither** to dry up – 6 **to remain** to be left – 7 **wisp** a thin
and weak blade of grass – 12 **seed** *Samen* – 13 **comfort** ['kʌmfət] consolation
(Trost) – 16 **to slam around** to make loud noises – 19 **he rides his fences** he
patrols his land – **dazed** as if hit on the head – 20 **to wince** to move back in
pain – **rib-thin** so thin that the ribs (= *Rippen*) show

Give Up on Wheat

Ma says,
"Try putting in a pond, Bayard.
We can fill it off the windmill.
5 We've got a good well."

Daddy grumbles, "The water'll seep
back into the ground
as fast as I can pump it, Pol.
We'll dry up our well
10 and then we'll have nothing."

"Plant some other things, then," Ma says.
"Try cotton,
sorghum. If we plant the fields in different crops,
maybe some will do better,
15 better than wheat."

Daddy says,
"No.
It has to be wheat.
I've grown it before.
20 I'll grow it again."

But Ma says, "Can't you see
what's happening, Bayard?
The wheat's not meant to be here."

And Daddy says,
25 "What about those apple trees of yours, Pol?
You think they are?
Nothing needs more to drink than those two.
But you wouldn't hear of leveling your apples,
would you?"

---

3 **pond** small area of water *(Teich)* – 5 **well** deep water hole in the ground
(Brunnen) – 6 **to grumble** to complain – **to seep** to sink into the ground –
13 **sorghum** ['sɔːgəm] grain growing in warm climates *(Hirse, Sorghum)* – 28 **to
level** *here:* to cut down – **apples** *here:* apple trees

Ma is bittering. I can see it in her mouth.
"A pond would work," she says,
sounding crusty and stubborn.

And Daddy says, "Look it, Pol, who's the farmer?
You or me?"

Ma says,
"Who pays the bills?"

"No one right now," Daddy says.

Ma starts to quaking but she won't let Daddy see.
Instead, she goes out to the chickens
and
her anger,
simmering over like a pot in an empty kitchen,
boils itself down doing chores.

April 1934

What I Don't Know

My teacher, Miss Freeland,
is singing
at the Shrine
along with famous
opera stars
from all around the country
in a play called
Madame Butterfly.

I've never heard of that play.

---

1 **bittering** *(non-standard)* becoming bitter – 3 **crusty** impatient, irritable *(gereizt)* – 7 **bill** a list ot things bought, etc., showing the sum of money one has to pay – 9 **she starts to quaking** *(non-standard)* she starts to quake, to shake – 13 **to simmer** to boil at a low temperature – 14 **chore** work done in the house – 19 **Shrine** name of an auditorium – 24 *Madame Butterfly* opera by Puccini

"Most everyone's heard of *Madame Butterfly*,"
Mad Dog says.

How does that
singing plowboy know something I don't?
5   And how much more is out there
most everyone else has heard of
except me?

April 1934

Apple Blossoms

10 Ma
has been nursing these two trees
for as long as I can remember.
In spite of the dust,
in spite of the drought,
15 because of Ma's stubborn care,
these trees are
thick with blossoms,
delicate and
pinky-white.

20 My eyes can't get enough of the sight of them.
I stand under the trees
and let the petals
fall into my hair,
a blizzard
25 of sweet-smelling flowers,
dropped from the boughs of the two
placed there

---

9 **blossom** flower of a tree – 11 **to nurse** to take care of as one would of a baby –
13 **in spite of** *trotz* – 18 **delicate** ['delɪkət] very fine, easily damaged – 22 **petal**
['petl] part of a flower *(Blütenblatt)* – 24 **blizzard** ['blɪzəd] snow storm –
26 **bough** [baʊ] branch *(Ast)*

in the front yard by Ma
before I was born,
that she and they might bring forth fruit
into our home,
together.

May 1934

World War

Daddy was just seventeen
when he fought in the
Great War off in France.

There's not much he's willing to
say about those days, except about the poppies.
He remembers the poppies,
red on the graves of the dead.

Daddy says
that war tore France up
worse than a tornado,
worse than a dust storm,
but no matter,
the wild poppies bloomed in the trail of the fighting,
brightening the French countryside.

I wish I could see poppies
growing out of this dust.

May 1934

---

1 **yard** (AE) garden – 3 **to bring forth** to produce – 10 **Great War** World War I
(1914–1918); the United States entered the war in 1917 – 12 **poppy** summer
flower *(Mohnblume)* – 16 **to tear** (tore, torn) to rip apart *(zerreißen)* – 19 **no
matter** nevertheless, in spite of that – 20 **to bloom** to be in flower – **trail** rough
path across open country – **in the trail of** after

Apples

Ma's apple blossoms
have turned to hard green balls.

To eat them now,
5   so tart,
would turn my mouth inside out,
would make my stomach groan.

But in just a couple months,
after the baby is born,
10   those apples will be ready
and we'll make pies
and sauce
and pudding
and dumplings
15   and cake
and cobbler
and have just plain apples to take to school
and slice with my pocket knife
and eat one juicy piece at a time
20   until my mouth is clean
and fresh
and my breath is nothing but apple.

June 1934

Dust and Rain

25   On Sunday,
winds came,

---

5 **tart** sour – 7 **to groan** to make a low, long sound when in pain – 8 **a couple months** *(informal)* a couple of months – 14 **dumpling** *here:* apple covered in dough *(=Teig)* and cooked – 16 **cobbler** fruit pie – 17 **plain** ordinary; *here:* uncooked

bringing a red dust
like prairie fire,
hot and peppery,
searing the inside of my nose,
the whites of my eyes.
Roaring dust,
turning the day from sunlight to midnight.

And as the dust left,
rain came.
Rain that was no blessing.
It came too hard,
too fast,
and washed the soil away,
washed the wheat away with it.
Now
little remains of Daddy's hard work.
And the only choice he has
is to give up or
start all over again.

At the Strong ranch
they didn't get a single drop.
So who fared better?

Ma looks out the window at her apple trees.
Hard green balls have dropped to the ground.
But there are enough left;
enough
for a small harvest,
if we lose no more.

June 1934

_____

4 **to sear** to burn – 6 **to roar** to make a loud noise (like a lion) – 10 **blessing**
Segen – 13 **soil** upper layer of the earth in which plants grow *(Boden)* – 16 **to
remain** to be left – 22 **to fare better** to be better off

Harvest

The combines have started moving across the fields,
bringing in wheat,
whatever has managed to grow.

5 Mr. Tuttle delivered the first load to town
selling it for seventy-three cents a bushel.
Not bad.

Mr. Chaffin, Mr. Haverstick, and Mr. French,
they've delivered their harvest too,
10 dropping it at the Joyce City grain elevator.

Daddy asked Mr. Haverstick how things looked
and Mr. Haverstick said he figures
he took eight bushels off a twenty-bushel acre.

If Daddy gets five bushels to his acre
15 it'll be a miracle.

June 1934

On the Road with Arley

Here's the way I figure it.
My place in the world is at the piano.
20 I'm earning a little money playing,
thanks to Arley Wanderdale.
He and his Black Mesa Boys have connections in
Keyes and Goodwell and Texhoma.

---

2 **combine (harvester)** ['kɒmbaɪn] machine that cuts the wheat and separates
the grains from the rest of the plant *(Mähdrescher)* – 5 **to deliver** to send –
6 **bushel** ['bʊʃl] U.S. unit of volume, equal to 35.24 liters – 10 **grain elevator**
Getreidesilo – 12 **to figure** ['fɪgə] to think – 13 **acre** 4047 square meters –
twenty-bushel acre an acre that would normally produce twenty bushels of
grain – 15 **miracle** ['mɪrəkl] s.th. wonderful and unexpected *(Wunder)*

And every little crowd
is grateful to hear a rag or two played
on the piano
by a long-legged, red-haired girl,
even when the piano has a few keys soured by dust.

At first Ma crossed her arms
against her chest
and stared me down,
hard-jawed and sharp, and said I couldn't go.
But the money helped convince her,
and the compliment from Arley and his wife, Vera,
that they'd surely bring my ma along to play too,
if she wasn't so far gone with a baby coming.
Ma said
okay,
but only for the summer,
and only if she didn't hear me gripe how I was tired,
or see me dragging my back end around,
or have to call me twice upon a morning,
or find my farm chores falling down,
and only if Arley's wife, Vera, kept an eye on me.

Arley says my piano playing is good.
I play a set of songs with the word baby in the title,
like "My Baby Just Cares for Me"
and "Walking My Baby Back Home."
I picked those songs on purpose for Ma,
and the folks that come to hear Arley's band,
they like them fine.

Arley pays in dimes.
Ma's putting my earnings away I don't know where,
saving it to send me to school in a few years.

---

2 **rag** piece of ragtime music from the turn of the century – 7 **chest** upper body –
9 **jaw** bone into which the teeth are set *(Kiefer)* – 17 **to gripe** to complain –
18 **to drag one's back end around** to move very slowly – 31 **school** college

The money doesn't matter much to me.
I'd play for nothing.
When I'm with Arley's boys we forget the dust.
We are flying down the road in Arley's car,
5   singing,
laying our voices on top of the
beat Miller Rice plays on the back of Arley's seat,
and sometimes, Vera, up front, chirps crazy notes with
no words
10   and the sounds she makes seem just about amazing.

It's being part of all that,
being part of Arley's crowd I like so much,
being on the road,
being somewhere new and interesting.
15   We have a fine time.

And they let me play piano, too.

June 1934

---

8 **to chirp** to sing like a bird

Summer 1934

Hope in a Drizzle

Quarter inch of rain
is nothing to complain about.
It'll help the plants above ground,
and start the new seeds growing.

That quarter inch of rain did wonders for Ma, too,
who is ripe as a melon these days.
She has nothing to say to anyone anymore,
except how she aches for rain,
at breakfast,
at dinner,
all day,
all night,
she aches for rain.

Today, she stood out in the drizzle
hidden from the road,
and from Daddy,
and she thought from me,
but I could see her from the barn,
she was bare as a pear,
raindrops
sliding down her skin,
leaving traces of mud on her face and her long back,
trickling dark and light paths,
slow tracks of wet dust down the bulge of her belly.
My dazzling ma, round and ripe and striped
like a melon.

July 1934

---

1 **drizzle** soft rain *(Nieselregen)* – 2 **quarter inch** about 0.6 cms – 9 **to ache for**
[eɪk] *here:* to long for – 20 **bare** naked – 23 **trace** mark *Spur* – 24 **to trickle** to
flow slowly – 25 **track** path – **bulge** big round lump – 26 **dazzling** brilliant

Dionne Quintuplets

While the dust blew
down our road,
against our house,
5   across our fields,
up in Canada
a lady named Elzire Dionne
gave birth to five baby girls
all at once.

10   I looked at Ma,
so pregnant with one baby.
"Can you imagine five?" I said.
Ma lowered herself into a chair.
Tears dropping on her tight stretched belly,
15   she wept
just to think of it.

July 1934

Wild Boy of the Road

A boy came by the house today,
20   he asked for food.
He couldn't pay anything, but Ma set him down
and gave him biscuits
and milk.
He offered to work for his meal,
25   Ma sent him out to see Daddy.
The boy and Daddy came back late in the afternoon.

---

1 **quintuplets** [kwɪnˈtʌplɔts] five babies born by the same mother at the same time – 14 **tight** *prall*

The boy walked two steps behind,
in Daddy's dust.
He wasn't more than sixteen.
Thin as a fence rail.
I wondered what
Livie Killian's brother looked like now.
I wondered about Livie herself.
Daddy asked if the boy wanted a bath,
a haircut,
a change of clothes before he moved on.
The boy nodded.
I never heard him say more than "Yes, sir" or
"No, sir" or
"Much obliged."

We watched him walk away
down the road,
in a pair of Daddy's mended overalls,
his legs like willow limbs,
his arms like reeds.
Ma rested her hands on her heavy stomach,
Daddy rested his chin on the top of my head.
"His mother is worrying about him," Ma said.
"His mother is wishing her boy would come home."

Lots of mothers wishing that these days,
while their sons walk to California,
where rain comes,
and the color green doesn't seem like such a miracle,
and hope rises daily, like sap in a stem.

---

4 **rail** horizontal bar, part of a fence – 11 **to nod** to move one's head up and down *(nicken)* – 14 **much obliged** thank you – 17 **to mend** to repair – 18 **willow** tree *(Weide)* – **limbs** [lɪmz] *here:* branches – 19 **reeds** leaves of grass – 21 **chin** part of the face *(Kinn)* – 28 **sap** liquid in a plant – **stem** part of a plant *(Halm)*

And I think, some day I'm going to walk there too,
through New Mexico and Arizona and Nevada.
Some day I'll leave behind the wind, and the dust
and walk my way West
5 and make myself to home in that distant place
of green vines and promise.

July 1934

The Accident

I got
10 burned
bad.

Daddy
put a pail of kerosene
next to the stove
15 and Ma,
fixing breakfast,
thinking the pail was
filled with water,
lifted it,
20 to make Daddy's coffee,
poured it,
but instead of making coffee,
Ma made a rope of fire.
It rose up from the stove
25 to the pail
and the kerosene burst
into flames.

---

6 **vine** climbing plant (producing grapes) – 13 **pail** (AE) bucket (BE) – 14 **stove**
apparatus used for cooking *(Herd)* – 16 **to fix** to make – 23 **rope** piece of thick,
strong string *(Seil, Tau)* – 26 **to burst into flames** to catch fire

Ma ran across the kitchen,
out the porch door,
screaming for Daddy.
I tore after her,
then,
thinking of the burning pail
left behind in the bone-dry kitchen,
I flew back and grabbed it,
throwing it out the door.

I didn't know.
I didn't know Ma was coming back.

The flaming oil
splashed
onto her apron,
and Ma,
suddenly Ma,
was a column of fire.
I pushed her to the ground,
desperate to save her,
desperate to save the baby, I
tried,
beating out the flames with my hands.
I did the best I could.
But it was no good.
Ma
got
burned
bad.

July 1934

---

2 **porch** verandah – 4 **to tear** (tore, torn) *here:* to run at great speed – 8 **to grab** to seize, to take – 17 **column** ['kɒləm] pillar *(Säule)* – 19 **desperate** ['despərət] eager

Burns

At first I felt no pain,
only heat.

I thought I might be swallowed by the heat,
5 like the witch in "Hansel and Gretel,"
and nothing would be left of me.

Someone brought Doc Rice.
He tended Ma first,
then came to me.
10 The doctor cut away the skin on my hands, it hung in
crested strips.
He cut my skin away with scissors,
then poked my hands with pins to see what I could feel.
He bathed my burns in antiseptic.

15 Only then the pain came.

July 1934

Nightmare

I am awake now,
still shaking from my dream:

20 I was coming home
through a howling dust storm,
my lowered face was scrubbed raw by dirt and wind.
Grit scratched my eyes,
it crunched between my teeth.

---

4 **to swallow** to eat up – 8 **to tend** to treat – 11 **crested** sticking out like the feathers on he head of some birds – 13 **to poke** to touch with a stick, pin, etc. – 14 **to bathe** [beɪð] to put into liquid – 15 **only then** *erst dann* – 17 **nightmare** *Albtraum* – 23 **grit** small pieces of sand

Sand chafed inside my clothes,
against my skin.
Dust crept inside my ears, up my nose,
down my throat.
I shuddered, nasty with dust.

In the house,
dust blew through the cracks in the walls,
it covered the floorboards and
heaped against the doors.
It floated in the air, everywhere.
I didn't care about anyone, anything, only the piano.
Isearched for it,
found it under a mound of dust.
I was angry at Ma for letting in the dust.
I cleaned off the keys
but when I played,
a tortured sound came from the piano,
like someone shrieking.
I hit the keys with my fist, and the piano broke into
a hundred pieces.

Daddy called to me. He asked me to bring water,
Ma was thirsty.
I brought up a pail of fire and Ma drank it. She had
given birth to a baby of flames. The baby
burned at her side.

I ran away. To the Eatons' farm.
The house had been tractored out,
tipped off its foundation.

---

1 **to chafe** to rub – 3 **to creep** (crept, crept) to move slowly – 5 **to shudder** to
tremble with fear and horror – 10 **to float** to move around through air or water
(schweben) – 13 **mound** small hill – 17 **tortured** full of pain *(gequält)* – 18 **to
shriek** to cry loudly *(kreischen)* – 27 **tractored out** destroyed (when a farmer
could not pay the bank, a tractor was sent to destroy his farmhouse) –
28 **tipped off** thrown down from – **foundation** firm elements such as concrete
blocks on which houses are built *(Fundament)*

No one could live there.
Everywhere I looked were dunes of rippled dust.
The wind roared like fire.
The door to the house hung open and there was
5 dust inside
several feet deep.
And there was a piano.

The bench was gone, right through the floor.
The piano leaned toward me.
10 I stood and played.
The relief I felt to hear the sound of music after the sound
of the piano at home. . . .

I dragged the Eatons' piano through the dust
to our house,
15 but when I got it there I couldn't play. I had swollen
lumps for hands,
they dripped a sickly pus,
they swung stupidly from my wrists,
they stung with pain.

20 When I woke up, the part
about my hands
was real.

July 1934

---

8 **bench** piano seat for more than one person – 16 **lump** solid mass without a
regular shape *(Klumpen)* – 17 **to drip** to let fall in drops – **pus** *Eiter* – 18 **to
swing** (swung, swung) to move like a pendulum – 19 **to sting** (stung, stung) to
hurt *(stechen)*

A Tent of Pain

Daddy
has made a tent out of the sheet over Ma
so nothing will touch her skin,
what skin she has left.
I can't look at her,
I can't recognize her.
She smells like scorched meat.
Her body groaning there,
it looks nothing like my ma.
It doesn't even have a face.

Daddy brings her water,
and drips it inside the slit of her mouth
by squeezing a cloth.
She can't open her eyes,
she cries out
when the baby moves inside her,
otherwise she moans,
day and night.
I wish the dust would plug my ears
so I couldn't hear her.

July 1934

Drinking

Daddy found the money
Ma kept squirreled in the kitchen under the
threshold.

---

3 **sheet** cloth used to cover the mattress of a bed – 8 **scorched** burnt – 14 **to squeeze** to press hard – 18 **to moan** to make a long, low sound when in pain *(stöhnen)* – 20 **to plug** to fill, to stop – 26 **to squirrel** to hide (from squirrel = *Eichhörnchen*) – 27 **threshold** ['θreʃhəʊld] doorstep *(Schwelle)*

It wasn't very much.
But it was enough for him to get good and drunk.

He went out last night.
While Ma moaned and begged for water.
5 He drank up the emergency money
until it was gone.

I tried to help her.
I couldn't aim the dripping cloth into her mouth.
I couldn't squeeze.
10 It hurt the blisters on my hands to try.
I only made it worse for Ma. She cried
for the pain of the water running into her sores,
she cried for the water that
would not soothe her throat
15 and quench her thirst,
and the whole time
my father was in Guymon,
drinking.

July 1934

20 **Devoured**

Doc sent me outside to get water.
The day was so hot,
the house was so hot.
As I came out the door,
25 I saw the cloud descending.
It whirred like a thousand engines.

---

2 **to get good and drunk** to get completely drunk – 4 **to beg for** to ask urgently for – 10 **blister** painful swelling on the skin *(Blase)* – 12 **sore** wound – 14 **to soothe** [suːð] to calm – 15 **to quench one's thirst** to satisfy one's thirst by drinking *(Durst stillen)* – 20 **to devour** [dɪˈvaʊə] to eat very quickly – 25 **to descend** to come down – 26 **to whir** to make a series of regular sounds

It shifted shape as it came
settling first over Daddy's wheat.
Grasshoppers,
eating tassels, leaves, stalks.
Then coming closer to the house,
eating Ma's garden, the fence posts,
the laundry on the line, and then,
the grasshoppers came right over me,
descending on Ma's apple trees.
I climbed into the trees,
opening scabs on my tender hands,
grasshoppers clinging to me.
I tried beating them away.
But the grasshoppers ate every leaf,
they ate every piece of fruit.
Nothing left but a couple apple cores,
hanging from Ma's trees.
I couldn't tell her,
couldn't bring myself to say
her apples were gone.
I never had a chance.

Ma died that day
giving birth to my brother.

August 1934

Blame

My father's sister came to fetch my brother,
even as Ma's body cooled.

---

1 **to shift shape** to change one's form – 4 **tassel** flowering part of a plant –
7 **laundry** washing – 11 **scab** hardened crust of dried blood on a wound
(Schorf) – 12 **to cling to** (clung, clung) to hold on to – 16 **apple core** seeds in
the middle of an apple – 25 **to blame s.o. for s.th.** to hold s.o. responsible

She came to bring my brother back to Lubbock
to raise as her own,
but my brother died before Aunt Ellis got here.
She wouldn't even hold his little body.
5   She barely noticed me.
As soon as she found my brother dead,
she
had a talk with my father.
Then she turned around
10 and headed back to Lubbock.

The neighbor women came.
They wrapped my baby brother in a blanket
and placed him in Ma's bandaged arms.
We buried them together
15 on the rise Ma loved,
the one she gazed at from the kitchen window,
the one that looks out over the
dried-up Beaver River.

Reverend Bingham led the service.
20 He talked about Ma,
but what he said made no sense
and I could tell
he didn't truly know her,
he'd never even heard her play piano.
25 He asked my father
to name my baby brother.
My father, hunched over, said nothing.
I spoke up in my father's silence.
I told the reverend
30 my brother's name was Franklin.
Like our President.

---

2 **to raise a child** to bring up a child – 10 **to head back** to go back – 12 **to wrap in a blanket** to put a blanket around – 13 **to bandage** to tie a piece of cloth around s.o.'s wound – 15 **rise** small hill – 19 **reverend** minister, pastor – **service** *Gottesdienst*; *here:* funeral – 21 **truly** really – 27 **to hunch over** to bend forward

The women talked as they
scrubbed death from our house.
I
stayed in my room
silent on the iron bed,
listening to their voices.

"Billie Jo threw the pail,"
they said. "An accident,"
they said.
Under their words a finger pointed.

They didn't talk
about my father leaving kerosene by the stove.
They didn't say a word about my father
drinking himself
into a stupor
while Ma writhed, begging for water.
They only said,
Billie Jo threw the pail of kerosene.

August 1934

Birthday

I walk to town.
I don't look back over my shoulder
at the single grave
holding Ma and my little brother.
I am trying not to look back at anything.

---

5 **iron** [ˈaɪən] a metal *(Eisen)* – 10 **to point a finger at s.o.** to blame s.o. – 14 **to drink o.s. into a stupor** to drink so much one becomes unconscious – 16 **to writhe** [raɪð] to twist and turn violently because of pain – 23 **grave** place where a dead person is buried

Dust rises with each step,
there's a greasy smell to the air.
On either side of the road are
the carcasses of jackrabbits, small birds, field mice,
5   stretching out into the distance.

My father stares out across his land,
empty but for a few withered stalks
like the tufts on an old man's head.
I don't know if he thinks more of Ma,
10 or the wheat that used to grow here.

There is barely a blade of grass
swaying in the stinging wind,
there are only these
lumps of flesh
15 that once were hands long enough to span octaves,
swinging at my sides.

I come up quiet
and sit behind Arley Wanderdale's house,
where no one can see me, and lean my head back,
20 and close my eyes,
and listen to Arley play.

August 1934

Roots

President Roosevelt tells us to
25 plant trees. Trees will
break the wind. He says,

---

2 **greasy smell** smell of fat – 3 **either side** both sides – 4 **carcass** ['kɑːkəs] dead
body – 7 **but for** except for – 8 **tuft** bunch of hair, grass – 11 **blade of grass**
Grashalm – 12 **to sway** to move in the wind – 15 **to span octaves** to reach from
one piano key to the one that is an octave away – 23 **root** part of the tree that
is in the ground

trees
will end the drought,
the animals can take shelter there,
children can take shelter.
Trees have roots, he says.
They hold on to the land.

That's good advice, but
I'm not sure he understands the problem.

Trees have never been at home here.
They're just not meant to be here.
Maybe none of us are meant to be here,
only the prairie grass
and the hawks.

My father will stay, no matter what,
he's stubborn as sod.
He and the land have a hold on each other.
But what about me?

August 1934

The Empty Spaces

I don't know my father anymore.
He sits across from me,
he looks like my father,
he chews his food like my father,
he brushes his dusty hair back
like my father,
but he is a stranger.

---

3 **to take shelter** to go to a place where one is protected – 11 **none** not any –
13 **hawk** large bird of prey *(Habicht)* – 15 **sod** top part of the soil with grass
and roots – 19 **space** place

I am awkward with him,
and irritated,
and I want to be alone
but I am terrified of being alone.

5 We are both changing,
we are shifting to fill in the empty spaces left by Ma.
I keep my raw and stinging hands
behind my back when he comes near
because he
10 stares
when he sees them.

September 1934

The Hole

The heat from the cookstove hurts my burns,
15 and the salt,
the water, and the dust hurt too.
I spend all my time in pain,
and
my father spends his time out the side of the house,
20 digging a hole,
forty feet by sixty feet,
six feet deep.

I think he is digging the pond,
to feed off the windmill,
25 the one Ma wanted,
but he doesn't say. He just digs.

---

1 **awkward** uncomfortable – 2 **irritated** made angry, annoyed – 4 **terrified** full
of fear – 21 **forty feet by sixty feet** 40 feet (c. 12 meters) wide and 60 feet (c. 18
meters) long

He sends me to the train yard to gather boards,
boards that once were boxcars
but now are junk.
I bring them back, careful of the scabs and the
raw sores on my bare hands.
I don't know what he needs boards for.
He doesn't tell me.

When he's not in the hole, digging,
he works on the windmill,
replacing the parts
that kept it from turning.

People stop by and watch. They think my father is crazy
digging such a big hole.
I think he's crazy too.
The water will seep back into the earth.
It'll never stay put in any old pond.
But my father has thought through all that
and he's digging anyway.

I think to talk to Ma about it,
and then I remember.

I can almost forgive him the taking of Ma's money,
I can almost forgive him his night in Guymon,
getting drunk.
But as long as I live,
no matter how big a hole he digs,
I can't forgive him that pail of kerosene
left by the side of the stove.

September 1934

---

2 **boxcar** an enclosed and covered railway car in which goods are carried –
3 **junk** worthless material – 10 **to replace** to exchange, to put in – 11 **to keep
s.th. from doing s.th.** to make it impossible for s.th. to do s.th.– 16 **to stay put**
to stay in the same place – 25 **no matter** *unabhängig davon, ganz egal*

Kilauea

A volcano erupted in Hawaii.
Kilauea.
It threw huge
5 chunks
into the air,
the ground shook,
and smoke
choked everything in its path.

10 ... sounds a little
like a dust storm.

September 1934

Boxes

In my closet are two boxes,
15 the gatherings of my life,
papers,
school drawings,
a broken hairpin,
a dress from my baby days,
20 my first lock of hair,
a tiny basket woven from prairie grass,
a doll with a china head,
a pink ball,
three dozen marbles,
25 a fan from Baxter's Funeral Home,
my baby teeth in a glass jar,
a torn map of the world,

---

1 **Kilauea** [ˌkiːlaʊˈeɪə] – 5 **chunk** large piece of s.th. – 9 **to choke** to kill by making breathing impossible – 14 **closet** [ˈklɒzɪt] wardrobe – 21 **to weave** (wove, woven) *weben* – 22 **china** porcelain – 24 **marble** glass ball *(Murmel)* – 25 **fan** *Fächer*

two candy wrappers,
a thousand things I haven't looked at
in years.
I kept promising to go through the boxes
with Ma
and get rid of what I didn't need,
but I never got to it
and now my hands hurt.
And I haven't got the heart.

September 1934

Night Bloomer

Mrs. Brown's
cereus plant bloomed on Saturday night.
She sent word
after promising I could come see it.
I rubbed my gritty eyes with swollen hands.
My stomach grizzled as I
made my way through the dark
to her house.
Ma wouldn't have let me go at all.
My father just stood in the doorway and
watched me leave.

It was almost three in the morning when I got there.
A small crowd stood around.
Mrs. Brown said,
"The blossom opened at midnight,
big as a dinner plate.
It took only moments to unfold."

---

1 **wrapper** paper used to cover s.th. – 6 **to get rid of** to throw out – 7 **to get to s.th.** to manage to do s.th. – 13 **cereus** ['sɪrɪəs] tropical cactus that blooms at night – 14 **to send word** to inform – 17 **to grizzle** to make a complaining noise

How can such a flower
find a way to bloom in this drought,
in this wind.

It blossomed at night,
5   when the sun couldn't scorch it,
when the wind was quiet,
when there might have been a sip of dew
to freshen it.

I couldn't watch at dawn,
10   when the flower,
touched by the first finger of morning light,
wilted and died.
I couldn't watch
as the tender petals burned up in the sun.

15   *September 1934*

The Path of Our Sorrow

Miss Freeland said,
"During the Great War we fed the world.
We couldn't grow enough wheat
20   to fill all the bellies.
The price the world paid for our wheat
was so high
it swelled our wallets
and our heads,
25   and we bought bigger tractors,
more acres,

---

7 **sip** a small quantity of liquid – 9 **dawn** time of day when light first appears –
12 **to wilt** to become dry – 14 **tender** weak, fragile – 16 **sorrow** deep sadness –
18 **to feed** (fed, fed) to give food to – 23 **wallet** (AE) purse (BE)

until we had mortgages
and rent
and bills
beyond reason,
but we all felt so useful, we didn't notice.
Then the war ended and before long,
Europe didn't need our wheat anymore,
they could grow their own.
But we needed Europe's money
to pay our mortgage,
our rent,
our bills.
We squeezed more cattle,
more sheep,
onto less land,
and they grazed down the stubble
till they reached root.
And the price of wheat kept dropping
so we had to grow more bushels
to make the same amount of money we made before,
to pay for all that equipment, all that land,
and the more sod we plowed up,
the drier things got,
because the water that used to collect there
under the grass,
biding its time,
keeping things alive through the dry spells
wasn't there anymore.

---

1 **mortgage** ['mɔːgɪdʒ] loan, money from the bank *(Hypothek)* – 2 **rent** money
paid to the owner of land one works but does not own – 3 **bill** written statement
of money that one owes for goods received *(Rechnung)* – 4 **beyond reason**
more than makes sense – 6 **before long** soon – 13 **to squeeze** *here:* to force into
a narrow space – **cattle** cows and bulls – 16 **stubble** parts left after corn has
been cut *(Stoppeln)* – 19 **to grow** *here:* to produce – 21 **equipment** machinery –
22 **the more ... the drier** *je mehr ... desto trockener* – 26 **to bide one's time** to
wait for the right moment to do s.th. – 27 **spell** period

Without the sod the water vanished,
the soil turned to dust.
Until the wind took it,
lifting it up and carrying it away.
5 Such a sorrow doesn't come suddenly,
there are a thousand steps to take
before you get there."
But now,
sorrow climbs up our front steps,
10 big as Texas, and we didn't even see it coming,
even though it'd been making its way straight for us
all along.

September 1934

---

1 **to vanish** ['vænɪʃ] to disappear – 12 **all along** all the time

---

Hired Work

My father hired on
at Wireless Power on Tuesday,
excavating for towers.

He said,
"I'm good at digging,"
and everyone who knows about our hole
knows he's telling the truth.

He might as well earn a couple dollars.
It doesn't look good for the winter crop.
Earning some cash will make him feel better.
I don't think he'll drink it up.
He hasn't done that since Ma.

It's hard to believe I once brought money in too,
even if it was just a dime now and then,
for playing piano.
Now I can't hardly stay in the same room with one.
Especially Ma's.

October 1934

Almost Rain

It almost rained Saturday.
The clouds hung low over the farm.
The air felt thick.
It smelled like rain.

---

2 **to hire on** to take a job – 3 **Wireless Power** a company running a radio
station – 4 **to excavate** to dig holes – **tower** tower used to transmit radio signals

In town,
the sidewalks
got damp.
That was all.

5 *November 1934*

Those Hands

The Wildcats started practice this week.
Coach Albright used to say I could play for the team.
"You've got what it takes, Billie Jo.
10 Look at the size of those hands," he'd say. "Look at how tall."
I'd tell him, "Just because I'm tall doesn't mean I can
play basketball,
or even that I want to."
But he'd say I should play anyway.

15 Coach Albright didn't say anything to me about
basketball this year.
I haven't gotten any shorter.
It's because of my hands.

My father used to say, why not put those hands to good use?
20 He doesn't say anything about "those hands"
anymore.
Only Arley Wanderdale talks about them,
and how they could play piano again,
if I would only try.

November 1934

---

7 **Wildcats** school basketball team – 19 **to put s.th. to good use** to use s.th. in
such a way that you profit from it

Real Snow

The dust stopped,
and it
snowed.
Real snow.
Dreamy Christmas snow,
gentle,
nothing blowing,
such calm,
like after a fever,
wet,
clinging to the earth,
melting into the dirt,
snow.

Oh, the grass, and the wheat
and the cattle,
and the rabbits,
and my father will be happy.

November 1934

Dance Revue

Vera Wanderdale
is putting on a dance revue at the Palace
and Arley asked
if I'd play a number with the Black Mesa Boys.
It's hard, coming on to Christmas,
just me and my father,
with no Ma and no little brother.
I don't really feel like doing anything.

---

7 **gentle** soft – 10 **fever** a disease involving a very high body temperature – 12 **to cling to** (clung, clung) to hold on to

Still, I told Arley I would try,
just because it looked like it meant a lot to him.
He said he'd be dancing then,
so he needed a piano player,
5   and Mad Dog would be singing,
and he knew how I'd just love to be
connected with anything Mad Dog's doing.

The costumes Vera ordered
come all the way from the city, she said.
10   Special,
the latest cuts.
I wish I could go with her
to pick them up.

During rehearsals,
15   Mad Dog comes off the stage after his numbers
and stands by the piano.
He doesn't look at me like
I'm a poor motherless thing.
He doesn't stare at my deformed hands.
20   He looks at me like I am
someone he knows,
someone named Billie Jo Kelby.
I'm grateful for that,
especially considering how bad I'm playing.

25   *December 1934*

Mad Dog's Tale

Mad Dog is surrounded by girls.
They ask him how he got his name.
He says, "It's not because I'm wild,

---

24 **considering** when seeing *(wenn man bedenkt)*

or a crazy, untamed boy,
but because fourteen years ago when I was two
I would bite anything I could catch hold of: my ma,
my brother, Doc Rice, even Reverend Bingham.
So my father named me Mad Dog.
And it stuck."

When I go home
I ask my father if he knows Mad Dog's
real name.
He looks at me like I'm talking in another language.

Ma could have told me.

December 1934

Art Exhibit

We had an art exhibit last week
in the basement of the courthouse,
to benefit the library.
Price of admission was one book
or ten cents.
I paid ten cents the first time,
but they let me in the second and third times for free.
That was awful kind,
since I didn't have another dime
and I couldn't bring myself to
hand over Ma's book of poetry
from the shelf over the piano.

It was really something to see the oil paintings,
the watercolors,

---

1 **untamed** wild – 6 **to stick** (stuck, stuck) *here:* to stay, to keep – 13 **art exhibit** [ɪgˈzɪbɪt] exhibition, art show – 15 **basement** (AE) cellar (BE) – **courthouse** *Gerichtsgebäude* – 16 **to benefit** [ˈbenɪfɪt] *here:* to raise money for – 17 **admission** *here:* ticket *(Eintritt)* – 21 **awful kind** awfully kind, very kind – 25 **shelf** *Regalbrett* – 26 **it was really something** it was something special

the pastels and charcoals.
There were pictures of the Panhandle in the old days
with the grass blowing and wolves,
there was a painting of a woman getting dressed
5 in a room of curtains,
and a drawing of a railroad station
with a garden out the front,
and a sketch of a little girl holding an enormous cat
in her lap.

10 But now the exhibit is gone,
the paintings
stored away in spare rooms
or locked up
where no one can see them.
15 I feel such a hunger
to see such things.
And such an anger
because I can't.

December 1934

---

1 **charcoal** *here:* drawing made with charcoal *(Kohlezeichnung)* – 8 **sketch** a
simple, not very detailed drawing – 12 **stored away** put away – **spare** extra

Winter 1935

State Tests Again

Miss Freeland said
our grade
topped the entire state of Oklahoma
on the state tests again, twenty-four
points higher
than the state average.

Wish I could run home and tell Ma
and see her nod
and hear her say,

"I knew you could."

It would be enough.

January 1935

Christmas Dinner Without the Cranberry Sauce

Miss Freeland
was my ma
at the school
Christmas dinner.

I thought I'd be
the only one
without a
real ma,
but two other motherless girls came.

---

3 **grade** class – 4 **to top** to be at the top – **entire** [ɪn'taɪə] whole – 7 **average** ['ævərɪdʒ] *Durchschnitt* – 14 **cranberry** red berry *(Preiselbeere)*

We served turkey,
chestnut dressing,
sweet potatoes, and brown gravy.
Made it all ourselves
5 and it came out
pretty good,
better than the Christmas dinner I made for my father
at home,
where we sat at the table,
10 silent, just the two of us.

Being there without Ma,
without the baby,
wouldn't have been so bad,
if I'd just remembered the cranberry sauce.
15 My father loved Ma's special cranberry sauce.
But she never showed me how to make it.

January 1935

Driving the Cows

Dust
20 piles up like snow
across the prairie,
dunes leaning against fences,
mountains of dust pushing over barns.
Joe De La Flor can't afford to feed his cows,
25 can't afford to sell them.
County Agent Dewey comes,
takes the cows behind the barn,
and shoots them.

---

1 **turkey** traditional Christmas meal *(Truthahn)* – 2 **chestnut** ['tʃesnʌt] *Esskastanie* – 3 **gravy** the juices that drip from cooking meat *(Soße)*

Too hard to
watch their lungs clog with dust,
like our chickens, suffocated.
Better to let the government take them,
than suffer the sight of their bony hides
sinking down
into the earth.

Joe De La Flor
rides the range.
Come spring he'll gather Russian thistle,
pulling the plant while it's still green and young,
before the prickles form, before it breaks free
to tumble across the plains.
He gathers thistle to feed what's left of his cattle,
his bone-thin cattle,
cattle he drives away from the dried-up Beaver River,
to where the Cimarron still runs,
pushing the herd across the breaks,
where they might last another week, maybe two,
until it
rains.

January 1935

First Rain

Sunday night,
I stretch my legs in my iron bed
under the roof.

---

2 **to clog** to block *(verkleben)* – 3 **suffocated** dead because of lack of air –
4 **hide** animal skin – 9 **to ride the range** to ride across the open country –
10 **come spring** when spring comes – **thistle** ['θɪsl] thorny plant *(Distel)* –
12 **prickle** thorn *(Dorne)* – 13 **to tumble** to roll – 18 **breaks** patches of land
where nothing grows

I place a wet cloth over my nose to keep
from breathing dust
and wipe the grime tracings from around my mouth,
and shiver, thinking of Ma.
5   I am kept company by the sound of my heart
drumming.

Restless,
I tangle in the dusty sheets,
sending the sand flying,
10 cursing the grit against my skin,
between my teeth,
under my lids,
swearing I'll leave this forsaken place.

I hear the first drops.
15 Like the tapping of a stranger
at the door of a dream,
the rain changes everything.
It strokes the roof,
streaking the dusty tin,
20 ponging,
a concert of rain notes,
spilling from gutters,
gushing through gullies,
soaking into the thirsty earth outside.

25 Monday morning dawns,
cloaked in mist.
I button into my dress, slip on my sweater,
and push my way off the porch,

---

3 **grime** dirt – **tracing** line *(Spur)* – 8 **to tangle** to be twisted *(verknotet sein)* –
10 **to curse** to damn *(verfluchen)* – 13 **forsaken** damned *(gottverlassen)* – 15 **to
tap** to make a knocking noise – 18 **to stroke** *streicheln* – 19 **to streak** to form
stripes – **tin** a metal *(Zinn)*, the roof is made of tin – 22 **to spill** *überfließen* –
gutter edge of the road where rain water collects – 23 **to gush** to flow with great
force – 24 **to soak** *here:* to sink – 26 **cloaked** covered – **mist** fog

sticking my face into the fog,
into the moist skin of the fog.
The sound of dripping surrounds me as I
walk to town.

Soaked to my underwear,
I can't bear to go
through the schoolhouse door,
I want only to stand in the rain.

Monday afternoon,
Joe De La Flor brushes mud from his horse,
Mr. Kincannon hires my father
to pull his Olds out of the muck on Route 64.

And later,
when the clouds lift,
the farmers, surveying their fields,
nod their heads as
the frail stalks revive,
everyone, everything, grateful for this moment,
free of the
weight of dust.

January 1935

Haydon P. Nye

Haydon P. Nye died this week.
I knew him to wave,
he liked the way I played piano.

2 **moist** damp, not dry – 5 **soaked** *here:* wet through and through – 12 **Olds**
Oldsmobile, brand name – **muck** mud – **Route 64** road going through the
Oklahoma Panhandle – 15 **to survey** to look over – 17 **frail** thin, weak –
18 **grateful** thankful – 20 **weight** s.th. heavy that presses you down *(Last)*

The newspaper said when Haydon first came
he could see only grass,
grass and wild horses and wolves roaming.

Then folks moved in and sod got busted
5 and bushels of wheat turned the plains to gold,
and Haydon P. Nye
grabbed the Oklahoma Panhandle in his fist
and held on.

By the time the railroad came in
10 on land Haydon sold them,
the buffalo and the wild horses had gone.

Some years
Haydon Nye saw the sun dry up his crop,
saw the grasshoppers chew it down,
15 but then came years of rain
and the wheat thrived,
and his pockets filled,
and his big laugh came easy.

They buried Haydon Nye on his land,
20 busted more sod to lay down his bones.
Will they sow wheat on his grave,
where the buffalo
once grazed?

January 1935

25 **Scrubbing Up Dust**

Walking past the Crystal Hotel
I saw Jim Martin down on his knees.

---

3 **to roam** to wander around – 4 **busted** broken up (by plows) – 16 **to thrive** to
grow well – 21 **to sow** [səʊ] to throw seed on the land *(säen)* – 25 **to scrub** to
rub hard in order to clean

He was scraping up mud that had
dried to crust
after the rain mixed with dust Sunday last.

When I got home
I took a good look at the steps
and the porch
and the windows.
I saw them with Ma's eyes and thought about
how she'd been haunting me.

I thought about Ma,
who would've washed clothes,
beaten furniture,
aired rugs,
scrubbed floors,
down on her knees,
brush in hand,
breaking that mud
like the farmers break sod,
always watching over her shoulder
for the next duster to roll in.

My stubborn ma,
she'd be doing it all
with my brother Franklin to tend to.
She never could stand a mess.
My father doesn't notice the dried mud.
Least he never tells me,
not that he tells me much of anything these days.
With Ma gone,
if the mud's to be busted,
the job falls to me.

---

1 **to scrape up** to rub to make s.th. smooth *(abkratzen)* – 9 **to haunt** to visit
(said of a ghost); *here:* to appear in one's thoughts – 13 **to air** to put out into
the air – 20 **duster** *here:* dust storm – 23 **to tend to s.o.** to take care of s.o. –
26 **least** at least *(wenigstens)*

It isn't the work I hate,
the knuckle-breaking work of beating mud out of
every blessed thing,
but every day
5   my fingers and hands
ache so bad. I think
I should just let them rest,
let the dust rest,
let the world rest.
10 But I can't leave it rest,
on account of Ma,
haunting.

January 1935

Outlined by Dust

15 My father stares at me
while I sit across from him at the table,
while I wash dishes in the basin,
my back to him,
the picked and festered bits of my hands in agony.
20 He stares at me
as I empty the wash water at the roots
of Ma's apple trees.

He spends long days
digging for the electric-train folks
25 when they can use him,
or working here,
nursing along the wheat,
what there is of it,
or digging the pond.

---

2 **knuckle-breaking** very hard – 3 **blessed** ['blesɪd] sacred, holy; *here:* damned –
11 **on account of** because of – 19 **picked** *here:* open – **festered** festering *(eitrig)* –
agony ['ægənɪ] great pain – 27 **to nurse** to take care of as one would of a baby

He sings sometimes under his breath,
even now,
even after so much sorrow.
He sings a man's song,
deep with what has happened to us.
It doesn't swing lightly
the way Ma's voice did,
the way Miss Freeland's voice does,
the way Mad Dog sings.
My father's voice starts and stops,
like a car short of gas,
like an engine choked with dust,
but then he clears his throat
and the song starts up again.

He rubs his eyes
the way I do,
with his palms out.
Ma never did that.
And he wipes the milk from his
upper lip same as me,
with his thumb and forefinger.
Ma never did that, either.

We don't talk much.
My father never was a talker.
Ma's dying hasn't changed that.
I guess he gets the sound out of him with the
songs he sings.

I can't help thinking
how it is for him,
without Ma.
Waking up alone, only
his shape
left in the bed,

_____

32 **shape** form

outlined by dust.
He always smelled a little like her
first thing in the morning,
  when he left her in bed
5 and went out to do the milking.
She'd scuff into the kitchen a few minutes later,
bleary eyed,
to start breakfast.
I don't think she was ever
10 really meant for farm life,
I think once she had bigger dreams,
but she made herself over
to fit my father.

Now he smells of dust
15 and coffee,
tobacco and cows.
None of the musky woman smell left that was Ma.

He stares at me,
maybe he is looking for Ma.
20 He won't find her.
I look like him,
I stand like him,
I walk across the kitchen floor
with that long-legged walk
25 of his.
I can't make myself over the way Ma did.

And yet, if I could look in the mirror and see her in my face.
If I could somehow know that Ma
and baby Franklin
30 lived on in me . . .

---

6 **to scuff** to scrape the feet *(schlurfen)* – 7 **bleary** (of eyes) red and unable to
see well – 10 **to be meant for** to be destined for *(bestimmt sein für)* – 12 **to
make o.s. over** to change – 17 **musky** smelling like musk (substance used for
perfumes)

But it can't be.
I'm my father's daughter.

January 1935

The President's Ball

All across the land,
couples dancing,
arm in arm, hand in hand,
at the Birthday Ball.

My father puts on his best overalls,
I wear my Sunday dress,
the one with the white collar,
and we walk to town
to the Legion Hall
and join the dance. Our feet flying,
me and my father,
on the wooden floor whirling
to Arley Wanderdale and the Black Mesa Boys.

Till ten,
when Arley stands up from the piano,
to announce we raised thirty-three dollars
for infantile paralysis,
a little better than last year.

And I remember last year,
when Ma was alive and we were
crazy excited about the baby coming.
And I played at this same party for Franklin D. Roosevelt

---

13 **Legion** the American Legion, a society, organized in 1919, composed of veterans of the armed forces – 16 **to whirl** to turn round and round – 20 **to announce** to make known publicly – **to raise** to collect – 21 **infantile paralysis** ['ɪnfəntaɪl pə'ræləsɪs] polio *(Kinderlähmung)*

and Joyce City
and Arley.

Tonight, for a little while
in the bright hall folks were almost free,
5 almost free of dust,
almost free of debt,
almost free of fields of withered wheat.
Most of the night I think I smiled.
And twice my father laughed.
10 Imagine.

January 1935

Lunch

No one's going hungry at school today.
The government
15 sent canned meat,
rice,
potatoes.
The bakery
sent loaves of bread,
20 and
Scotty Moore, George Nall, and Willie Harkins
brought in milk,
fresh creamy milk
straight from their farms.
25 Real lunch and then
stomachs
full and feeling fine
for classes
in the afternoon.

---

15 **canned meat** meat in cans (AE), tins (BE)

The little ones drank themselves into white
mustaches,
they ate
and ate,
until pushing back from their desks,
their stomachs round,
they swore they'd never eat again.

The older girls,
Elizabeth and LoRaine, helped Miss Freeland
cook,
and Hillary and I,
we served and washed,
our ears ringing with the sound of satisfied children.

February 1935

Guests

In our classroom this morning,
we came in to find a family no one knew.

They were shy,
a little frightened,
embarrassed.
A man and his wife, pretty far along with a baby coming,

a baby
coming

two little kids
and a grandma.
They'd moved into our classroom during the night.

---

2 **mustache** ['mʌstæʃ] hair growing above the upper lip – 13 **to ring with** to
echo – **satisfied** happy, content – 20 **embarrassed** self-conscious, awkward

An iron bed
and some pasteboard boxes. That's all they had.
They'd cleaned the room first, and arranged it,
making a private place for themselves.

5 "I'm on the look for a job," the man said.
"The dust blew so mean last night
I thought to shelter my family here awhile."

The two little kids turned their big eyes
from Miss Freeland
10 back to their father.

"I can't have my wife sleeping in the cold truck,
not now. Not with the baby coming so soon."

Miss Freeland said they could stay
as long as they wanted.

15 *February 1935*

Family School

Every day we bring fixings for soup
and put a big pot on to simmer.
We share it at lunch with our guests,
20 the family of migrants who have moved out from dust
and Depression
and moved into our classroom.
We are careful to take only so much to eat,
making sure there's enough soup left in the pot for
25 their supper.

---

2 **pasteboard** strong paper, cardboard *(Pappe)* – 7 **to shelter** to protect, to give
a roof over their heads – 17 **fixings** *(informal)* ingredients, things used for –
18 **to simmer** to cook gently just at boiling point – 21 **Depression** Great
Depression, period of economic problems in the U.S. 1929–1939

Some of us bring in toys
and clothes for the children.
I found a few things of my brother's
and brought them to school,
little feed-sack nighties,
so small,
so full of hope.

Franklin
never wore a one of the nighties Ma made him,
except the one we buried him in.

The man, Buddy Williams,
helps out around the school,
fixing windows and doors,
and the bad spot on the steps,
cleaning up the school yard
so it never looked so good.

The grandma takes care of the children,
bringing them out when the dust isn't blowing,
letting them chase tumbleweeds across the field
behind the school,
but when the dust blows,
the family sits in their little apartment inside our classroom,
studying Miss Freeland's lessons
right alongside us.

February 1935

---

9 **a one** *(informal)* a single one – 19 **to chase** to run after – **tumbleweed**
western prairie plant that breaks off and is rolled about by the wind

Birth

One morning when I arrive at school
Miss Freeland says to keep the kids out,
that the baby is coming
5 and no one can enter the building
until the birthing is done.
I think about Ma
and how that birth went.
I keep the kids out and listen behind me,
10 praying for the sound of a baby
crying into this world,
and not the silence
my brother brought with him.
And then the cry comes
15 and I have to go away for a little while
and just walk off the feelings.

Miss Freeland rings the bell to call us in
but I'm not ready to come back yet.
When I do come,
20 I study how fine that baby girl is. How perfect,
and that she is wearing a feed-sack nightgown that
was my brother's.

February 1935

Time to Go

25 They left a couple weeks after the baby came,
all of them crammed inside that rusty old truck.
I ran half a mile in their dust to catch them.
I didn't want to let that baby go.

---

26 **crammed** close together in a small space *(vollgestopft)*

"Wait for me," I cried,
choking on the cloud that rose behind them.
But they didn't hear me.
They were heading west.
And no one was looking back.

February 1935

Something Sweet from Moonshine

Ashby Durwin
and his pal Rush
had themselves a
fine operation on the Cimarron River,
where the water still runs a little,
though the fish are mostly dead
from the dust floating on the surface.
Ashby and Rush were cooking up moonshine
in their giant metal still on the bank
when Sheriff Robertson caught them.
He found jugs of finished whiskey,
and barrels and barrels of mash,
he found two sacks of rye,
and he found sugar,
one thousand pounds of sugar.

The government men took Ashby and Rush off to Enid
for breaking the law,
but Sheriff Robertson stayed behind,
took apart the still,

---

7 **moonshine** *(slang)* illegally made alcoholic drink – 9 **pal** friend – 14 **surface** outer or topmost part *(Oberfläche)* – 16 **still** apparatus used for distilling alcoholic drinks – 18 **jug** container with handle and lip *(Krug)* – 19 **barrel** container used for holding liquids *(Fass)* – **mash** mixture from which alcohol can be distilled – 20 **rye** kind of grain *(Roggen)* – 23 **Enid** large city in northern Oklahoma – 26 **to take apart** to break, to destroy

washed away the whiskey and the mash,
and thought about that sugar,
all that sugar, one-half ton of sugar.
Sheriff decided
5   some should find its way
into the mouths of us kids.
Bake for them, Miss Freeland, he said,
bake them cakes and cookies and pies,
cook them custard and cobbler and crisp,
10 make them candy and taffy and apple pandowdy.

Apple pandowdy!

These kids,
Sheriff Robertson said,
ought to have something sweet to
15 wash down their dusty milk.
And so we did.

February 1935

Dreams

Each day after class lets out,
20 each morning before it begins,
I sit at the school piano
and make my hands work.
In spite of the pain,
in spite of the stiffness
25 and scars.
I make my hands play piano.
I have practiced my best piece over and over
till my arms throb,

---

9 **custard** dessert made from milk, sugar and eggs – **crisp** a dessert of fruit
baked with a sweet crumbly topping – 10 **taffy** candy made with brown sugar –
pandowdy pudding made with apples – 28 **to throb** to beat

because Thursday night
the Palace Theatre is having a contest.
Any man, woman, or child
who sings,
dances,
reads,
or plays worth a lick
can climb onto that stage.
Just register by four P.M.
and give them a taste of what you can do
and you're in,
performing for the crowd,
warming up the audience for the
Hazel Hurd Players.
I figure if I practice enough
I won't shame myself.
And we sure could use the extra cash
if I won.
Three-dollar first prize,
two-dollar second,
one-dollar third.
But I don't know if I could win anything,
not anymore.
It's the playing I want most,
the proving I can still do it.
without Arley making excuses.
I have a hunger,
for more than food.
I have a hunger
bigger than Joyce City.
I want tongues to tie, and
eyes to shine at me

---

2 **contest** ['kɒntest] competition – 7 **lick** *(informal)* small amount – 9 **to register** to put one's name down – 10 **taste** *here:* idea – 12 **to perform** to act on stage – 15 **to figure** ['fɪgə] to think – 31 **to tie tongues** to make speechless

87

like they do at Mad Dog Craddock.
Course they never will,
not with my hands all scarred up,
looking like the earth itself,
5 all parched and rough and cracking,
but if I played right enough,
maybe they would see past my hands.
Maybe they could feel at ease with me again,
and maybe then,
10 I could feel at ease with myself.

February 1935

The Competition

I suppose everyone in Joyce City and beyond,
all the way to Felt
15 and Keyes
and even Guymon,
came to watch the talent show at the Palace,
Thursday night.

Backstage,
20 we were seventeen amateur acts,
our wild hearts pounding,
our lips sticking to our teeth,
our urge to empty ourselves
top and bottom,
25 made a sorry sight
in front of the
famous Hazel Hurd Players.

---

5 **parched** dried up, hard – 8 **at ease** relaxed – 14 **Felt, Keyes, Guymon** towns
in the Oklahoma Panhandle – 21 **to pound** to beat – 23 **urge** need, desire –
25 **to make a sorry sight** to look bad so that people feel sorry

But they were kind to us,
helped us with our makeup and our hair,
showed us where to stand,
how to bow,
and the quickest route to the
toilet.

The audience hummed on the other side of the
closed curtain,
Ivy Huxford
kept peeking out and giving reports
of who was there,
and how she never saw so many seats
filled in the Palace,
and that she didn't think they could
squeeze a
rattlesnake
into the back
even if he paid full price,
the place was so packed.

My father told me he'd come
once chores were done.
I guess he did.

The Grover boys led us off.
They worked a charm,
Baby on the sax,
Jake on the banjo,
and Ben on the clarinet.
The Baker family followed, playing
just like they do at home
every night after dinner.
They didn't look nervous at all.

---

7 **to hum** to make a steady noise *(summen)* – 15 **to squeeze into** to press in
firmly – 24 **to work a charm** to fascinate

The tap dancers,
they rattled the teeth in their jaws
and the eyeballs in their skulls,
their feet flying,
5 their arms swinging,
their mouths gapping.
Then Sunny Lee Hallem
tumbled and leaped onto the stage,
the sweat flying off her,
10 spotting the Palace floor.
Marsh Worton struggled out,
his accordion leading the way.
George and Agnes Harkins ran their fingers over the
strings of their harps,
15 made you want to look up into the heavens for angels,
but only scenery
and lights
and ropes and sandbags hung overhead,
and then there was me on piano.

20 I went on somewhere near the backside of middle,
getting more and more jittery with each act,
till my time came.
I played "Bye, Bye, Blackbird"
my own way,
25 messing with the tempo,
and the first part sounded like
I used just my elbows,
but the middle sounded good
and the end,
30

---

1 **tap dancer** *Stepptänzer* – 3 **skull** bone part of the head *(Schädel)* – 8 **to leap**
to jump – 10 **to spot** to make spots on – 14 **string** part of a musical instrument
(Saite) – **harp** *Harfe* – 16 **scenery** background for the stage – 20 **I went on ...
middle** it was my turn near the end of the first half – 21 **jittery** nervous – 25 **to
mess with** to play around with, to change deliberately

I forgot I was even playing
in front of the packed Palace Theatre.
I dropped right inside the music and
didn't feel anything
till after
when the clapping started
and that's when I noticed my hands hurting
straight up to my shoulders.
But the applause
made me forget the pain,
the audience roared when I finished,
they came to their feet,
and I got third prize,
one dollar,
while Mad Dog Craddock, singing,
won second,
and Ben Grover
and his crazy clarinet
took first.

The tap dancers pouted into their mirrors,
peeling off their makeup and their smiles.
Birdie Jasper claimed
it was all my fault she didn't win,
that the judges were just being nice to a cripple,
but the harpin' Harkins were kind
and the Hazel Hurd Players
wrapped their long arms around me
and said I was swell
and in the sweaty dim chaos backstage
I ignored the pain running up and down my arms,
I felt like I was part of something grand.

---

20 **to pout** to stick out one's lips because one is dissatisfied *(schmollen)* – 21 **to peel off** to take off – 22 **to claim** to say *(behaupten)* – 28 **swell** *(informal)* wonderful – 29 **dim** dark – 31 **grand** important

But they had to give my ribbon and my dollar to my father,
'cause I couldn't hold
anything in my hands.

February 1935

5   **The Piano Player**

Arley says,
"We're
doing a show at the school in a week, Billie Jo.
Come play with us."

10   If I asked my father
he'd say yes.
It's okay with him if I want to play.
He didn't even know I was at the piano again till the other night.
He's making some kind of effort to get on
15   better with me now,
Since I "did him proud" at the Palace.

But I say, "No."

It's too soon after the contest.
It still hurts too much.

20   Arley doesn't understand.
"Just practice more," he says.
"You'll get it back,
you can travel with us again this summer
if you'd like."

25   I don't say
it hurts like the parched earth with each note.
I don't say,

---

14 **to make an effort** to try hard – **to get on with s.o.** to be on good terms with
s.o. *(mit jdm. auskommen)* – 16 **did him proud** made him proud

one chord and
my hands scream with pain for days.
I don't show him
the swelling
or my tears.

I tell him, "I'll try."

At home, I sit at
Ma's piano,
I don't touch the keys.
I don't know why.

I play "Stormy Weather" in my mind,
following the phrases in my imagination,
saving strength,
so that when I sit down at a piano that is not Ma's,
when everyone crowds into the school
for Arley's show,
no one can say
that Billie Jo Kelby plays like a cripple.

March 1935

No Good

I did play like a cripple at Arley's show,
not that Arley would ever say it.
But my hands are no good anymore,
my playing's no good.
Arley understands, I think.
He won't ask again.

March 1935

---

11 **Stormy Weather** popular song written in 1933 – 12 **imagination** mind

Snow

Had to check
yesterday morning
to make sure that was
5   snow
on the ground,
not dust.
But you can't make a dustball
pack together
10 and slam against the side of the barn, and
echo across the fields.
So I know
it was snow.

March 1935

15 ## Night School

My father thought maybe
he ought to go to night school,
so if the farm failed
there'd be prospects to fall back on.
20 He's starting to sound like Ma.

"The farm won't fail," I tell him.
"Long as we get some good rain."
I'm starting to sound like him.

"It's mostly ladies in those classes," he says,
25 "they take bookkeeping and civics,
and something called business English."

---

2 **to check** to find out if something is correct – 4 **to make sure** to see, to be certain – 10 **to slam** to throw hard – 11 **echo** ['ekəʊ] – 18 **to fail** to go bankrupt – 19 **prospects** chances in the future – **to fall back on s.th.** to turn to s.th. for help – 22 **long as** *(informal)* as long as – 25 **civics** social studies

I can't imagine him
taking any of those things.
But maybe he doesn't care so much about the classes.
Maybe he's thinking more about the company of ladies.

I'll bet none of the ladies mind
spending time with my father,
he's still good looking
with his strong back,
and his blondy-red hair
and his high cheeks rugged with wind.

I shouldn't mind either.
It's dinner I don't have to
come up with,
'cause the ladies bring chicken and biscuits for him.
I'm glad to get out of cooking.
Sometimes with my hands,
it's hard to keep the fire,
wash the pans,
hold the knife, and spread a little butter.
But I do mind his spending time with all those biddies.

I turn my back on him as he goes,
and settle myself in the parlor
and touch Ma's piano.

My fingers leave sighs
in the dust.

March 1935

---

5 **to mind** to have s.th. against – 10 **rugged** ['rʌgɪd] rough – 20 **biddies** *(slang)* women – 22 **to settle** to sit down – 24 **sigh** low tone of worry *(Seufzer)*

Dust Pneumonia

Two Fridays ago,
Pete Guymon drove in with a
truck full of produce.
5 He joked with Calb Hardly,
Mr. Hardly's son,
while they unloaded eggs and cream
down at the store.
Pete Guymon teased Calb Hardly about the Wildcats
10 losing to Hooker.
Calb Hardly teased Pete Guymon about his wheezy truck
sucking in dust.

Last Friday,
Pete Guymon took ill with dust pneumonia.
15 Nobody knew how to keep that produce truck on the road.
It sat,
filled with turkeys and heavy hens
waiting for delivery,
it sat out in front of Pete's drafty shack,
20 and sits there still,
the cream curdling
the apples going soft.

Because a couple of hours ago,
Pete Guymon died.
25 Mr. Hardly
was already on the phone to a new produce supplier,
before evening.

---

1 **pneumonia** [n(j)uːˈməʊnɪə] *Lungenentzündung* – 4 **produce** [ˈprɒdjuːs] farm
goods – 9 **to tease** to make fun of – 11 **wheezy** producing a whistling sound –
12 **to suck in** to breathe in *(einsaugen)* – 18 **delivery** taking goods to s.o.'s
house – 19 **drafty** *zugig* – 21 **to curdle** to go sour – 26 **supplier** person or firm
that delivers goods to stores *(Lieferant)*

He had people in his store
and no food to sell them.

His boy, Calb,
slammed the basketball against the side of the house
until Calb's ma yelled for him to quit,
and late that night a truck rattled up to the store,
with colored springs,
dozens of hens,
filthy eggs,
and a driver with no interest whatsoever in young
Calb Hardly
or his precious Wildcats.

March 1935

Dust Storm

I never would have gone to see the show
if I had known a storm like this would come.
I didn't know when going in,
but coming out
a darker night I'd never seen.
I bumped into a box beside the Palace door
and scraped my shins,
then tripped on something in my path,
I don't know what,
and walked into a phone pole,
bruised my cheek.

The first car that I met was sideways in the road.
Bowed down, my eyes near shut,

---

5 **to yell** to cry out loud, to shout – **to quit** to stop – 9 **filthy** very dirty – 10 **no interest whatsoever** no interest at all – 12 **precious** ['preʃəs] of great value *(kostbar)* – 21 **shin** lower part of the leg *(Schienbein)* – 22 **to trip** to stumble *(stolpern)* – 25 **to bruise** [bru:z] to hurt – 27 **to bow** [baʊ] to lower the body

trying to keep the dust out,
I saw its headlights just before I reached them.

The driver called me over and I felt my way,
following his voice.
5 He asked me how I kept the road.
"I feel it with my feet," I shouted over the
roaring wind,
"I walk along the edge.
One foot on the road, one on the shoulder."
10 And desperate to get home,
he straightened out his car,
and straddled tires on the road and off,
and slowly pulled away.

I kept along. I know that there were others
15 on the road,
from time to time I'd hear someone cry out,
their voices rose like ghosts on the howling wind;
no one could see. I stopped at neighbors'
just to catch my breath
20 and made my way from town
out to our farm.
Everyone said to stay
but I guessed
my father would
25 come out to find me
if I didn't show,
and get himself lost in the
raging dust and maybe die
and I
30 didn't want that burden on my soul.

---

9 **shoulder** edge of the road – 11 **to straighten out** to put straight on the road –
12 **to straddle tires on the road and off** to have two tires on the road and two
on the shoulder – 13 **to pull away** to drive off – 19 **to catch one's breath** [breθ]
to start to breathe regularly again – 30 **burden** a heavy weight that presses you
down *(Last)*

Brown earth rained down
from sky.
I could not catch my breath
the way the dust pressed on my chest
and wouldn't stop.
The dirt blew down so thick
it scratched my eyes
and stung my tender skin,
it plugged my nose and filled inside my mouth.
No matter how I pressed my lips together,
the dust made muddy tracks
across my tongue.

But I kept on,
spitting out mud,
covering my mouth,
clamping my nose,
the dust stinging the raw and open
stripes of scarring on my hands,
and after some three hours I made it home.

Inside I found my father's note
that said he'd gone to find me
and if I should get home, to just stay put.
I hollered out the front door
and the back;
he didn't hear,
I didn't think he would.
The wind took my voice and busted it
into a thousand pieces,
so small
the sound
blew out over Ma and Franklin's grave,
thinner than a sigh.

---

9 **to plug** to clog *(verstopfen)* – 14 **to spit out** (spat, spat) *ausspucken* – 16 **to clamp** to shut close

I waited for my father through the night, coughing up dust,
cleaning dust out of my ears,
rinsing my mouth, blowing mud out of my nose.

Joe De La Flor stopped by around four to tell me
5 they found one boy tangled in a barbed-wire fence,
another smothered in a drift of dust.

After Joe left I thought of the famous Lindberghs,
and how their baby was killed and never came back
to them.
10 I wondered if my father would come back.

He blew in around six A.M.
It hurt,
the sight of him
brown with dirt,
15 his eyes as red as raw meat,
his feet bruised from walking in worn shoes
stepping where he couldn't see
on things that bit and cut into his flesh.

I tried to scare up something we could eat,
20 but couldn't keep the table clear of dust.
Everything I set
down for our breakfast
was covered before we took a bite,
and so we chewed the grit and swallowed
25 and I thought of the cattle
dead from mud in their lungs,

---

3 **to rinse** to wash out – 4 to stop by to visit, to call on s.o. – 5 **tangled** caught
up in – **barbed wire** wire with sharp points, used to fence in cattle –
6 **smothered** dead because he couldn't breathe – 7 **Lindbergh** Charles (1902 –
1974), known for his first non-stop solo flight across the Atlantic in 1927; the
Lindberghs' baby was kidnapped in 1932 and murdered by the kidnappers –
11 **to blow in** to come in – 19 **to scare s.th. up** *(informal)* to find (usually s.th.
to eat) – 23 **to take a bite** to eat

and I thought of the tractor
buried up to the steering wheel,
and Pete Guymon,
and I couldn't even recognize the man
sitting across from me,
sagging in his chair,
his red hair gray and stiff with dust,
his face deep lines of dust,
his teeth streaked brown with dust.
I turned the plates and glasses upside down,
crawled into bed, and slept.

March 1935

Broken Promise

It rained
a little
everywhere
but here.

March 1935

Motherless

If Ma could put her arm across my shoulder
sometime,
or stroke back my hair,
or sing me to sleep, making the soft sounds,
the reassuring noises,
that no matter how brittle and sharp life seemed,

---

6 **to sag** to sink down – 17 **but** except *(außer)* – 24 **reassuring** [ˌriːəˈʃɔːrɪŋ] comforting *(beruhigend)* – 25 **brittle** *here:* difficult to deal with

no matter how brittle and sharp she seemed,
she was still my ma who loved me,
then I think I wouldn't be so eager to go.

March 1935

5 **Following in His Steps**

Haydon Parley Nye's wife,
Fonda,
died today,
two months after she lost her man.

10 The cause of death was
dust pneumonia,
but I think
she couldn't go on without Haydon.

When Ma died,
15 I didn't want to go on, either.
I don't know. I don't feel the same now,
not exactly.
Now that I see that one day
comes after another
20 and you get through them
one measure at a time.
But I'd like to go,
not like Fonda Nye,
I don't want to die,
25 I just want to go,
away,
out of the dust.

March 1935

---

21 **measure** [ˈmeʒə] *here:* step

Heartsick

The hard part is in spite of everything
if I had any boy court me,
it'd be Mad Dog Craddock.
But Mad Dog can have any girl.
Why would he want me?

I'm so restless.
My father asks what's going on with me.
I storm up to my room,
leaving him alone
standing in the kitchen.
If Ma was here
she would come up and listen.
And then later,
she would curl beside my father,
and assure him that everything was all right,
and soothe him into his farmer's sleep.

My father and I,
we can't soothe each other.
I'm too young,
he's too old,
and we don't know how to talk anymore
if we ever did.

April 1935

---

3 **to court** to try to win a woman's or a girl's attention *(den Hof machen)* – 15
to curl to snuggle up *(sich ankuscheln)* – 16 **to assure** to tell, to reassure – 17
to soothe [su:ð] to calm, to bring comfort

Skin

My father has a raised spot
on the side of his nose
that never was there before
5   and won't go away.
And there's another on his cheek
and two more on his neck,
and I wonder
why the heck is he fooling around.
10   He knows what it is.
His father had those spots too.

April 1935

Regrets

I never go by Arley's anymore.
15   Still,
every week
he comes to school to teach and
sometimes
I bump into Vera, or
20   Miller Rice,
or Mad Dog.

They are always kind.
They ask after my father.
They ask how my hands are feeling.
25   I cross my arms in front of me
tight
so my scars won't show.

---

2 **raised spot** swelling – 9 **the heck** *(informal) verflixt nochmal* – **is he fooling around** *here:* does he not go to the doctor – 19 **to bump into** to run into, to meet by chance

These days Mad Dog looks at me
halfway between picking a fight and kindness.
He walks with me a ways some afternoons,
never says a word.
He's quiet once the other girls go off.
I've had enough of quiet men.
I ought to keep clear of Mad Dog.
But I don't.

April 1935

Fire on the Rails

I hate fire.
Hate it.
But the entire Oklahoma Panhandle is so dry,
everything is going up in flames.
Everything too ready to ignite.
Last week
the school caught fire.
Damage was light,
on account of it being caught early.
Most kids joked about it next day,
but it terrified me.
I could hardly go back in the building.
And this week
three boxcars
in the train yard
burned to ash.
Jim Goin and Harry Kesler
spotted the fire,

---

2 **to pick a fight** to start or provoke a fight – 7 **to keep clear of** to stay away
from – 15 **to ignite** to catch fire – 19 **on account of** because – 21 **to terrify** to
frighten – 28 **to spot** to see, to discover

and that was a miracle
considering the fierceness of the dust storm
at the time.
The fire boys
5   tore over,
but they couldn't put the blaze out without water,
and water is exactly what they didn't have.
So they separated the burning cars
and moved them down a siding,
10   away from any little thing that might catch
if the flames hopped.
It was all they talked about at school.
The dust blew,
they say,
15   so you'd think it would have smothered the fire out,
but the flames,
crazy in the wind,
licked away at the wooden frames of the three boxcars,
until nothing remained but warped metal,
20   and twisted rails,
scorched dirt, and
charred ties.

No one talks about fire
right to my face.
25   They can't forget how fire changed my life.
But I hear them talking anyway.

April 1935

---

5 **to tear** (tore, torn) *here:* to rush – 6 **blaze** large fire – 9 **siding** railway track
off the main track – 19 **warped** bent, twisted, out of shape – 22 **charred** burnt
(verkohlt) – **tie** wooden log on which the rails rest *(Schwelle)*

The Mail Train

They promised
through rain,
heat,
snow,
and gloom
but they never said anything about dust.

And so the mail got stuck
for hours,
for days,
on the Santa Fe
because mountains of dust
had blown over the tracks,
because blizzards of dust
blocked the way.

And all that time,
as the dust beat down on the cars,
a letter was waiting inside a mail bag.
A letter from Aunt Ellis, my father's sister,
written just to me,
inviting me to live with her in Lubbock.
I want to get out of here,
but not to Aunt Ellis,
and not to Lubbock, Texas.
My father didn't say much when I asked
what I should do.
"Let's wait and see,"
he said.
What's that supposed to mean?

April 1935

---

2 **they promised** they said the mail would come no matter what happens –
6 **gloom** darkness and depression – 11 **Santa Fe** western railroad company

Migrants

We'll be back when the rain comes,
they say,
pulling away with all they own,
5   straining the springs of their motor cars.
Don't forget us.

And so they go,
fleeing the blowing dust,
fleeing the fields of brown-tipped wheat
10   barely ankle high,
and sparse as the hair on a dog's belly.

We'll be back, they say,
pulling away toward Texas,
Arkansas,
15   where they can rent a farm,
pull in enough cash,
maybe start again.

We'll be back when it rains,
they say,
20   setting out with their bedsprings and mattresses,
their cookstoves and dishes,
their kitchen tables,
and their milk goats
tied to their running boards
25   in rickety cages,
setting out for
California,

---

1 **migrants** ['maɪgrənts] people moving from one place to another – 4 **to own** to have – 5 **to strain the springs** die Federung belasten – 9 **brown-tipped** with brown, dried-up tops – 10 **ankle high** going up to the ankles (= Knöchel) – 11 **sparse** [spɑːs] growing at widely spaced intervals – 23 **goat** (Ziege) – 24 **running board** board below the door of an old-fashioned car (Trittbrett) – 25 **rickety** ['rɪkətɪ] not very stable, makeshift – **cage** structure in which animals are kept

where even though they say they'll come back,
they just might stay
if what they hear about that place is true.

Don't forget us, they say.
But there are so many leaving,
how can I remember them all?

April 1935

Blankets of Black

On the first clear day
we staggered out of our caves of dust
into the sunlight,
turning our faces to the big blue sky.

On the second clear day
we believed
the worst was over at last.
We flocked outside,
traded in town,
going to stores and coming out
only to find the air still clear
and gentle,
grateful for each easy breath.

On the third clear day
summer came in April
and the churches opened their arms to all comers
and all comers came.
After church,
folks headed for

---

1 **even though** although – 10 **to stagger** to walk unsteadily *(stolpern)* – **cave**
large hole in a cliff *(Höhle)* – 16 **to flock** to gather like a flock of sheep – 27 **to
head for** to go to

picnics,
car trips. No one could stay inside.

My father and I argued about the funeral
of Grandma Lucas,
5   who truly was no relation.
But we ended up going anyway,
driving down the road in a procession to Texhoma.

Six miles out of town the air turned cold,
birds beat their wings
10   everywhere you looked,
whole flocks
dropping out of the sky,
crowding on fence posts.
I was sulking in the truck beside my father
15   when
heaven's shadow crept across the plains,
a black cloud,
big and silent as Montana,
boiling on the horizon and
20   barreling toward us.
More birds tumbled from the sky
frantically keeping ahead of the dust.

We watched as the storm swallowed the light.
The sky turned from blue
25   to black,
night descended in an instant
and the dust was on us.

The wind screamed.
The blowing dirt ran

---

3 **to argue** to quarrel – 5 **truly** really – **relation** relative – 7 **Texhoma** see map p.
155 – 14 **to sulk** to refuse to speak because one is in a bad mood *(schmollen)* –
18 **Montana** big state in the northwestern U.S. – 19 **horizon** [hə'raɪzən] – 20 **to
barrel** to move at great speed – 22 **frantic** fearful, hurried, disordered –
26 **instant** moment

so thick
I couldn't see the brim of my hat
as we plunged from the truck,
fleeing.

The dust swarmed
like it had never swarmed before.

My father groped for my hand,
pulled me away from the truck.
We ran,
a blind pitching toward the shelter of a small house,
almost invisible,
our hands tight together,
running toward the ghostly door,
pounding on it with desperation.

A woman opened her home to us,
all of us,
not just me and my father,
but the entire funeral procession,
and one after another,
we tumbled inside, gasping,
our lungs burning for want of air.

All the lamps were lit against the dark,
the house dazed by dust,
gazed weakly out.
The walls shook in the howling wind.
We helped tack up sheets on the windows and doors
to keep the dust down.

Cars and trucks
unable to go on,

---

2 **brim** *Rand, Krempe* – 3 **to plunge** to dive *(tauchen); here:* to move at great speed – 5 **to swarm** to move in large quantities – 10 **pitching** violent move – 11 **invisible** not to be seen – 14 **to pound** to knock hard – **desperation** despair *(Verzweiflung)* – 20 **to gasp** to try to catch one's breath – 21 **want** lack, absence – 26 **to tack up** to hang up and fix

their ignitions shorted out by the static electricity,
opened up and let out more passengers,
who stumbled for shelter.
One family came in
5 clutched together,
their pa, divining the path
with a long wooden rod.

If it hadn't been for the company,
this storm would have broken us
10 completely,
broken us more thoroughly than
the plow had broken the Oklahoma sod,
more thoroughly than my burns
had broken the ease of my hands.
15 But for the sake of the crowd,
and the hospitality of the home that sheltered us,
we held on
and waited,
sitting or standing, breathing through wet cloths
20 as the fog of dust filled the room
and settled slowly over us.

When it let up a bit,
some went on to bury Grandma Lucas,
but my father and I,
25 we cleaned the thick layer of grime
off the truck,
pulled out of the procession and headed on home,
creeping slowly along the dust-mounded road.

---

1 **ignition** *Zündung* – **to short out** *kurzschließen* – 5 **to clutch** to cling to – 6 **to divine** to guess – 7 **rod** long thin pole – 8 **if it hadn't been for the company** if the other people hadn't been there – 11 **thorough** ['θʌrə] through and through *(gründlich)* – 15 **for the sake of** *um ... willen* – 16 **hospitality** kindness in welcoming strangers or guests *(Gastfreundschaft)* – 17 **to hold on** to survive – 22 **to let up** to calm down – 25 **layer** covering *(Schicht)* – 28 **mounded** covered with mounds, i.e. little hills

When we got back,
we found the barn half covered in dunes,
I couldn't tell which rise of dust was Ma and Franklin's grave.
The front door hung open,
blown in by the wind.
Dust lay two feet deep in ripply waves
across the parlor floor,
dust blanketed the cookstove,
the icebox,
the kitchen chairs,
everything deep in dust.
And the piano . . .
buried in dust.

While I started to shovel,
my father went out to the barn.
He came back, and when I asked, he said
the animals
weren't good,
and the tractor was dusted out,
and I said, "It's a wonder
the truck got us home."
I should have held my tongue.
When he tried starting the truck again,
it wouldn't turn over.

April 1935

---

6 **ripply waves** little waves caused by the wind – 24 **to turn over** *here:* to start
(said of an engine)

The Visit

Mad Dog came by
to see how we made out
after the duster.

5   He didn't come to court me.
I didn't think he had.

We visited more than an hour.
The sky cleared enough to see Black Mesa.
I showed him my father's pond.

10 Mad Dog said he was going to Amarillo,
to sing, on the radio,
and if he sang good enough,
they might give him a job there.

"You'd leave the farm?" I asked.
15 He nodded.
"You'd leave school?"
He shrugged.

Mad Dog scooped a handful of dust,
like a boy in a sandpit.
20 He said, "I love this land,
no matter what."

I looked at his hands.
They were scarless.

Mad Dog stayed longer than he planned.
25 He ran down the road
back to his father's farm when he realized the time.

---

3 **to make out** to manage – 7 **we visited** *here:* he stayed – 8 **Black Mesa** plateau
in northwestern Cimarron County that rises close to 5,000 feet (1,500 meters) –
17 **to shrug** to lift the shoulders in order to say "I don't know" – 18 **to scoop** to
take up in one's hands – 19 **sandpit** *here:* sandbox; place for little children to
play in

Dust rose each place his foot fell,
leaving a trace of him
long after he'd gone.

April 1935

Freak Show

The fellow from Canada,
James Kingsbury,
photographer from the *Toronto Star*,
way up there in Ontario,
the man who took the first pictures of
the Dionne Quintuplets,
left his homeland and
came to Joyce City
looking for some other piece of
oddness,
hoping to photograph the drought
and the dust storms
and
he did
with the help of Bill Rotterdaw
and Handy Poole,
who took him to the sandiest farms and
showed off the boniest cattle in the county.

Mr. Kingsbury's pictures of those Dionne babies
got them famous,
but it also got them taken from their
mother and father

---

5 **freak** a thing or event that is very abnormal – **freak show** an exhibition of freaks, i.e. physically deformed people or animals (formerly in circus side shows) – 9 **Ontario** province of Canada – 15 **oddness** strangeness

and put on display
like a freak show,
like a tent full of two-headed calves.
Now I'm wondering
5 what will happen to us
after he finishes taking pictures of our dust.

April 1935

Help from Uncle Sam

The government
10 is lending us money
to keep the farm going,
money to buy seed,
feed loans for our cow,
for our mule,
15 for the chickens still alive and the hog,
as well as a little bit of feed
for us.

My father was worried about
paying back,
20 because of what Ma had said,
but Mrs. Love,
the lady from FERA,
assured him he didn't need to pay a single cent
until the crops came in,
25 and if the crops never came, then he wouldn't pay a thing.

So my father said
okay.
Anything to keep going.

---

8 **Uncle Sam** the U.S. government – 13 **feed** food (usu. for animals) – 15 **hog** pig (AE) – 22 **FERA** Federal Emergency Relief Administration, a government organization

He put the paperwork on the shelf,
beside Ma's book of poetry
and the invitation from Aunt Ellis.
He just keeps that invitation from her,
glowering down at me from the shelf above the piano.

April 1935

Let Down

I was invited to graduation,
to play the piano.

I couldn't play.
It had been too long.
My hands wouldn't work.
I just sat on the piano bench,
staring down at the keys.
Everyone waited.
When the silence went on so long
folks started to whisper,
Arley Wanderdale lowered his head and
Miss Freeland started to cry.
I don't know,
I let them down.

I didn't cry.
Too stubborn.
I got up and walked off the stage.

I thought maybe if my father ever went to Doc Rice
to do something about the spots on his skin,
Doc could check my hands too,
tell me what to do about them.

---

1 **paperwork** forms to be filled out, contracts etc. – 5 **to glower** [ˈɡlaʊə] to look
at angrily – 7 **to let s.o. down** to disappoint s.o.

But my father isn't going to Doc Rice,
and now
I think we're both turning to dust.

May 1935

5 **Hope**

It started out as snow,
oh,
big flakes
floating
10 softly,
catching on my sweater,
lacy on the edges of my sleeves.

Snow covered the dust,
softened the
15 fences,
soothed the parched lips
of the land.

And then it changed,
halfway between snow and rain,
20 sleet,
glazing the earth.

Until at last
it slipped into rain,
light as mist.

25 It was the kindest
kind of rain
that fell.

---

12 **lacy** looking like lace *(= Spitzen)*, delicate – 20 **sleet** mixture of rain and snow– 21 **to glaze** to cover with s.th. shiny

Soft and then a little heavier,
helping along
what had already fallen
into the
hard-pan
earth
until it
rained,
steady as a good friend
who walks beside you,
not getting in your way,
staying with you through a hard time.

And because the rain came
so patient and slow at first,
and built up strength as the earth
remembered how to yield,
instead of washing off,
the water slid in,
into the dying ground
and softened its stubborn pride,
and eased it back toward life.

And then,
just when we thought it would end,
after three such gentle days,
the rain
came
slamming down,
tons of it,
soaking into the ready earth
to the primed and greedy earth,
and soaking deep.

---

16 **to yield** *here:* to receive the water – 21 **to ease** *here:* to move gently –
30 **primed** ready – **greedy** always wanting more *(gierig)*

It kept coming,
thunder booming,
lightning
kicking,
5   dancing from the heavens
down to the prairie,
and my father
dancing with it,
dancing outside in the drenching night
10   with the gutters racing,
with the earth puddled and pleased,
with my father's near-finished pond filling.

When the rain stopped,
my father splashed out to the barn,
15   and spent
two days and two nights
cleaning dust out of his tractor,
until he got it running again.
In the dark, headlights shining,
20   he idled toward the freshened fields,
certain the grass would grow again,
certain the weeds would grow again,
certain the wheat would grow again too.

May 1935

25   **The Rain's Gift**

The rain
has brought back some grass
and the ranchers
have put away the

---

9 **drenching** very wet – 10 **gutter** ditch at the side of a street that carries off
rain – 11 **puddled** covered with puddles *(Pfützen)* – 20 **to idle** to move slowly

feed cake
and sent their cattle
out to graze.
Joe De La Flor
5 is singing in his saddle again.

May 1935

Hope Smothered

While I washed up dinner dishes in the pan,
the wind came from the west
10 bringing—
dust.
I'd just stripped all the gummed tape from the windows.
Now I've got dust all over the clean dishes.

I can hardly make myself
15 get started cleaning again.

Mrs. Love is taking applications
for boys to do CCC work.
Any boy between eighteen and twenty-eight can join.
I'm too young
20 and the wrong sex
but what I wouldn't give to be
working for the CCC
somewhere far from here,
out of the dust.

May 1935

---

1 **feed cake** pressed-together hay, straw, etc., used to feed cattle when they can't
graze outside – 12 **to strip** to take away – **gummed tape** *Klebeband* –
16 **application** request to be allowed to work *(Bewerbung)* – 17 **CCC** Civilian
Conservation Corps, a government agency

Sunday Afternoon at the Amarillo Hotel

Everybody gathered at
the Joyce City Hardware and Furniture Company
on Sunday
5 to hear Mad Dog Craddock
sing on WDAG
from the Amarillo Hotel.
They hooked up speakers
and the sweet sound
10 of Mad Dog's voice
filled the creaky aisles.

Arley Wanderdale was in Amarillo with Mad Dog,
singing and playing the piano,
and the Black Mesa Boys were there
15 too.
I ached for not being there with them.

But there was nothing more most folks in Joyce City
wanted to do
than spend a half hour
20 leaning on counters,
sitting on stairs,
resting in chairs,
staring at the hardware
and the tableware,
25 listening to hometown boys
making big-time music
on the radio.

They kept time in the aisles,
hooting after each number,

<hr>

6 **WDAG** identification or "name" of the Amarillo radio station at the time –
8 **to hook up speakers** to connect loudspeakers – 11 **creaky** making a
squeaking sound (when you walk over floor boards) – 28 **to keep time** to
imitate the beat with hands and feet – 29 **to hoot** to cry out

and when Mad Dog finished his last song, they sent
the dust swirling,
cheering and whooping,
patting each other on the back,
as if they'd been featured
on WDAG themselves.

I tried cheering for Mad Dog with everyone else,
but my throat
felt like a trap had
snapped down on it.

That Mad Dog, he didn't have
a thing to worry about.
He sang good, all right.
He'll go far as he wants.

May 1935

Baby

Funny thing about babies.
Ma died having one,
the Lindberghs said good night to one and lost it,
and somebody
last Saturday
decided to
give one away.

Reverend Bingham says
that Harley Madden
was sweeping the dust out of church,

---

2 **to swirl** to move round and round – 3 **to whoop** to shout in a happy way –
5 **to be featured** ['fiːtʃəd] to be presented – 9 **trap** object for catching animals
(Falle) – 10 **to snap** to move quickly into a position *(zuschnappen)* – 14 **far as**
as far as

shining things up for Sunday service,
when he swept himself up to a package
on the north front steps.

He knelt,
5 studying the parcel,
and called to Reverend Bingham,
who came right by and opened the package up.

It held a living baby.
Reverend Bingham took it to Doc Rice.
10 Doc checked it, said it was fine,
only small,
less than a five-pound sack of sugar,
and a little cold from
spending time on the north front steps,
15 but Mrs. Bingham
and the reverend
warmed that baby with
blankets and sugar water,
and tender talk,
20 and the whole of Joyce City came forward with gifts.

I asked my father if we could adopt it,
but he said
we stood about as much chance
of getting that baby
25 as the wheat stood of growing,
since we couldn't give the baby anything
not even a ma.
Then he looked at me
sorry as dust.
30 And to make up for it,
he pulled out a box with the rest of the clothes

---

4 **to kneel** (knelt, knelt) [ni:l] to go down on one's knees – 19 **tender** soft,
gentle – 20 **to come forward** *here:* to offer

124

Ma had made for our new baby
and told me to drop them by the church if I wanted.

I found the dimes Ma'd been saving,
my earnings from the piano,
inside an envelope,
in the box of baby Franklin's nighties.
She had kept those dimes to send me
to Panhandle A and M.
To study music.

No point now.

I sat at her piano a long time after I
got back from the church,
imagining
a song for my little brother,
buried in Ma's arms on a knoll overlooking the
banks of the Beaver,
imagining a song for the Lindbergh baby
stiff in the woods,
imagining a song for this new baby
who
would not be my father's son.

May 1935

Old Bones

Once
dinosaurs roamed
in Cimarron County.

---

8 **Panhandle A and M** Agricultural and Mechanical College, today the
Oklahoma Panhandle State University in Goodwell – 10 **no point** useless –
15 **knoll** [nəʊl] low hill – 25 **dinosaur** [ˈdaɪnəsɔː] – **to roam** to wander about

Bones
showing
in the green shale,
ribs the size of plow blades,
5   hip bones like crank phones,
and legs running
like fence rails
down to a giant
foot.

10   A chill shoots up my spine
imagining a dinosaur
slogging out of an Oklahoma sea,
with turtles swimming around its legs.
I can see it sunning itself on the swampy banks,
15   beyond it a forest of ferns.
It's almost easy to imagine,
gazing out from our house
at the dust-crushed fields,
easy to imagine filling in all the emptiness with green,
20   easy to imagine such a beast
brushing an itchy rump against our barn.
But all that remains of it
is bone,
broken and turned to stone,
25   trapped in the hillside,
this once-upon-a-time real-live dinosaur
who lived,
and fed,

---

3 **shale** easily breakable rock composed of claylike sediments *(Schiefer)* – 4 **rib**
part of the chest *(Rippe)* – **blade** flat piece of metal with a sharp edge – 5 **crank
phone** phone with a crank *(= Kurbel)* – 8 **giant** [ˈdʒaɪənt] huge – 10 **chill** shiver
(Schüttelfrost) – **spine** bony part of the back *(Wirbelsäule)* – 12 **to slog** to
make a long and difficult journey – 13 **turtle** large reptile with a thick shell
(Schildkröte) – 14 **swampy** marshy *(sumpfig)* – 15 **fern** plant growing in the
woods *(Farn)* – 18 **dust-crushed** destroyed by dust – 21 **itchy** *(informal)*
juckend – **rump** upper part of the body *(Rumpf)*

and roamed
like a ridiculous
long-necked cow,
and then fell down and died.
I think for a moment of Joe De La Flor
herding brontosaurus instead of cattle
and I
smile.

I tell my father,
Let's go to the site
and watch the men chip away with ice picks,
let's see how they plaster the bones.
Please, before they ship the whole thing to Norman.

I am thinking
that a dinosaur is getting out of Joyce City
a hundred million years too late to
appreciate the trip,
and that I ought to get out before my own
bones turn to stone.
But I keep my thoughts to myself.

My father thinks awhile,
rubbing that spot on his neck.
He looks out the window,
out across the field,
toward the knoll where Ma and the baby lie.
"It's best to let the dead rest," he says.
And we stay home.

June 1935

---

2 **ridiculous** [rɪˈdɪkjʊləs] laughable – 6 **to herd** to watch animals – **brontosaurus**
special kind of dinosaur – 10 **site** place – 11 **to chip** to break off small quantities
at a time – 12 **to plaster** *here:* to put bone fragments together with the help of
plaster *(= Gips)* – 13 **Norman** city in central Oklahoma – 17 **to appreciate**
[əˈpriːʃɪeɪt] *here:* to enjoy

The Dream

Piano, my silent
           mother,
                      I can touch you,
5 you are cool
           and smooth
                and willing
to stay with me
           stay with me
10   talk to me.
Uncomplaining
           you accept
                the cover to your keys
and still
15   you
                make room
for all that I
           place
                there.
20 We close our eyes
           together
                and together find that stillness
like a pond
           a pond
25   when the wind is quiet
and the surface
           glazes
                gazing unblinking

---

28 **unblinking** constant, without closing one's eyes

at the blue sky.
                    I play songs
                              that have only the pattern
of my self in them
                    and you hum along
                              supporting me.
You are the
                    companion
                              to myself.
The mirror
                    with my mother's eyes.

July 1935

Midnight Truth

I am so filled with bitterness,
it comes from the dust, it comes
from the silence of my father, it comes
from the absence of Ma.

I could've loved her better.
She could've loved me, too.
But she's rock and dust and wind now,
she's carved stone,
she's holding my stone brother.

I have given my father so many chances
to understand, to
reach out, to
love me. He once did.
I remember his smile,
his easy talk.

---

3 **pattern** particular model to be followed *(Muster)* – 6 **to support** to help –
7 **companion** friend – 21 **to carve** to cut out *(schnitzen)*

Now there's nothing easy between us.
Sometimes he takes notice of me,
like coming after me in the dust.
But mostly I'm invisible.
5 Mostly I'm alone.

My father's digging his own grave,
he calls it a pond,
but I know what he's up to.
He is rotting away,
10 like his father,
ready to leave me behind in the dust.
Well, I'm leaving first.

July 1935

Out of the Dust

15 This is not a dream.
There's no comfort in dreams.
I try to contain the ache as I leave my bed,
I try to still my heart as I
slip from my room with my kerchief of dimes.
20 Moving slowly down the stairs,
I cross through the kitchen, taking only some biscuits,
and leave my father's house.
It's the middle of the night and I hear every sound
inside me, outside me.
25 I go,
knowing that I'll die if I stay,
that I'm slowly, surely
smothering.

---

9 **to rot** to die slowly *(verrotten)* – 17 **to contain** to keep within certain limits –
18 **to still** to calm – 19 **kerchief** scarf *(Halstuch)*

I walk through the calm night,
under the stars.
I walk to
where the train stops long enough
for a long-legged girl to latch on
and as my heart races
I feel the earth tremble beneath me and then
the sound of sharp knives,
metal against metal,
as the train pulls up to the station.
Once I might've headed east,
to Mr. Roosevelt.
Now I slip under cover of darkness
inside a boxcar
and let the train carry me west.
Out of the dust.

August 1935

Gone West

I am stiff and sore.
In two endless days on this train, I have
burned in the desert,
shivered in the mountains,
I have seen the
camps of dust-bowl migrants
along the tracks.

There was one girl.
I saw her through the slat in the boxcar.

---

5 **to latch on** *here:* to get on – 7 **beneath** under – 19 **to be sore** to ache – 27 **slat** a narrow strip of wood

She stared up at the passing train.
She stood by the tracks watching,
and I knew her.

August 1935

₅ **Something Lost, Something Gained**

He climbs into my car.
He's dirty and he has a sour smell.
His eyes are ringed by the soil that comes from riding trains.
But there's a deeper shadow to those eyes,
₁₀ like ashes,
like death.
He needs a hair comb and a shave,
and a mending needle applied to his pants.

He speaks to me,
₁₅ "Where you from, miss?" he wants to know.
He shows me a picture of his family.
A wife. Three boys.
The photograph is all he carries.
That and the shredding, stinking clothes on his back.
₂₀ I feed him two of the stale biscuits I've been hoarding
and save the rest.
I'll be hungry tonight,
what with giving my day's biscuits away.
But I can see the gaunt of hunger in his cheeks.
₂₅ He asks if I have water and I shake my head,
my tongue thick with thirst.

---

13 **mending** repairing – **to apply to** to use on – 19 **shredding** hanging in shreds,
torn – 20 **stale** old and dry – **to hoard** to save – 23 **what with giving** because I
have given – 24 **gaunt** gauntness, skinniness

He eats the biscuits.
He doesn't care they're caked with dust.
He finishes eating and crumbs stick to his mustache.
He's staring hard at me and his eyes water.
"I've done it again," he says.
"Taken food from a child."
I show him my cloth bag with more biscuits.
"At home," he said, "I couldn't feed them,
couldn't stand the baby always crying.
And my wife,
always that dark look following me.
Couldn't take no more.

Lost our land, they tractored us out so's we had to leave,
rented awhile, then moved in with Lucille's kin.
Couldn't make nothing grow."

I nodded. "I know."

We talked as the train rocked,
as the cars creaked,
as the miles showed nothing but empty space,
we talked through the pink of the setting sun,
and into the dark.
I told him about Ma dying.
I told him about my father,
and how the thing that scared us both the most
was being left alone.

And now I'd gone and left him.
I told him about the piano,
and Arley Wanderdale,
and how I wasn't certain of the date,

_____

13 **tractor s.o. out** to force farmers to leave their lands by destroying their houses with tractors – **so's we had to** *(non-standard)* so that we had to –
14 **kin** family

but I thought it might be my birthday,
but he was sleeping by then, I think.

He was like tumbleweed.
Ma had been tumbleweed too,
5   holding on for as long as she could,
then blowing away on the wind.

My father was more like the sod.
Steady, silent, and deep.
Holding on to life, with reserves underneath
10   to sustain him, and me,
and anyone else who came near.
My father
stayed rooted, even with my tests and my temper,
even with the double sorrow of
15   his grief and my own,
he had kept a home
until I broke it.

When I woke,
the man was gone, and so were my biscuits,
20   but under my hat I found the photograph of his family,
the wife and three boys.
Maybe the photograph was
left in trade for the biscuits,
maybe it was a birthday gift,
25   the one thing he had left to give.
The children in the picture were clean and serious,
looking out with a certain longing.
The baby had his eyes.

---

10 **to sustain** to support, to give strength to – 13 **test** *here:* bad temper,
moodiness – **temper** tendency to become angry – 23 **in trade** in exchange –
27 **longing** desire for s.th. that cannot be fulfilled *(Sehnsucht)*

On the back of the photograph,
in pencil,
was the address of his family in
Moline, Kansas.
First chance, I'd send the picture back,
let his wife know he was still alive.

I got off the train in Flagstaff, Arizona.
A lady from a government agency saw me.
She gave me water and food.
I called Mr. Hardly from her office and asked him to
let my father know . . .
I was coming home.

August 1935

Homeward Bound

Getting away,
it wasn't any better.
Just different.
And lonely.
Lonelier than the wind.
Emptier than the sky.
More silent than the dust,
piled in drifts between me
and my
father.

August 1935

---

14 **homeward bound** going home – 22 **piled** heaped up – **drift** a small hill like
a dune formed by the wind

Met

My father is waiting at the station
and I call him
Daddy
5   for the first time
since Ma died,
and we walk home,
together,
talking.
10 I tell him about getting out of the dust
and how I can't get out of something
that's inside me.
I tell him he is like the sod,
and I am like the wheat,
15 and I can't grow everywhere,
but I can grow here,
with a little rain,
with a little care,
with a little luck.
20 And I tell him how scared I am about those spots on his skin
and I see he's scared too.
"I can't be my own mother," I tell him,
"and I can't be my own father
and if you're both going to leave me,
25 well,
what am I supposed to do?"
And when I tell Daddy so,
he promises to call Doc Rice.

He says the pond is done.
30 We can swim in it once it fills,
and he'll stock it with fish too,

---

31 **to stock** to fill

catfish, that I can go out and
catch of an evening
and fry up.
He says I can even plant flowers,
if I want.

As we walk together,
side by side,
in the swell of dust,
I am forgiving him, step by step,
for the pail of kerosene.
As we walk together,
side by side,
in the sole-deep dust,
I am forgiving myself
for all the rest.

August 1935

---

1 **catfish** kind of freshwater fish *(Wels)* – 8 **swell** regular movement of waves –
13 **sole-deep** deep as the shoe soles

Cut It Deep

I went in with Daddy to see Doc Rice.
Doc said,
"Why'd you wait so long
to show someone those spots, Bayard?"
5   I scowled at Daddy.
He looked at the wall.
I think
he didn't care much,
if he had some cancer
10   and took and died.
Figured he'd see Ma then,
he'd see my brother.
It'd be out of his hands.
He'd be out of the dust.

15
Now he's going to wear bandages
where Doc cut the cancer out
the best he could.
And we have to wait
and hope Daddy didn't
20   get help too late.

I ask Doc about my hands.
"What," I say,
"can I do with them?"
Doc looks carefully at the mottled skin,
25   the stretched and striped and crackled skin.
"Quit picking at them," he says.

---

6 **to scowl** [skaʊl] to frown to show that one is angry – 11 **to take** *here:* to become sick, to fall ill – 25 **mottled** having different colors – 26 **crackled** *here:* cracked – 26 **to pick at** to touch repeatedly

"Rub some ointment in them before you go to bed," he says.
"And use them, Billie Jo," he says"
"They'll heal up fine if you just use them."

Daddy sits on my bed
and I open the boxes,
the two boxes
that have been in my closet
for years now.
The dust is over everything,
but I blow it off,
and Daddy is so quiet
when he sees
some of the things
that're still so strong of Ma,
and we end up keeping everything but a palmful
of broken doll dishes.
I thought once to go through these boxes with
Ma,
but Daddy is
sitting on the edge of my bed.
My mouth feels cottony.
I fix dinner
and Daddy tells me about
when he was a boy.

He says, "I wasn't always sure
about the wheat,
about the land,
about life in the Panhandle.
I dreamed of running off too,
though I never did.

---

1 **ointment** an oily, medicinal substance, salve *(Salbe)* – 3 **to heal** to get well –
15 **palmful** [ˈpɑːmfʊl] handful – 21 **cottony** dry, as if she had cotton wool
(= *Watte)* in her mouth

I didn't have half your sauce, Billie Jo," he says.
And it's the first time I ever knew
there was so much to the two of us,
so much more than our red hair
5 and our long legs
and the way we rub our eyes
when we're tired.

October 1935

The Other Woman

10 Her name is Louise,
she stayed by Daddy the days I was away.

The first time I met her she came to dinner bringing two
baskets of food.
She's a good cook
15 without showing off.

She has a way of making my father do things.
When Louise came to dinner,
Daddy got up and cleaned the kitchen when we were
done eating.
20 He tied an apron around his middle
and he looked silly as a cow
stuck in a hole,
but Louise ignored that,
and I took a lesson from her.

25 We walked around the farm
even though she'd probably already seen it
while I was gone.

---

1 **sauce** sauciness, rudeness; *here:* courage – 15 **to show off** to brag, to show
how good one is – 19 **we were done eating** we had finished our meal

She didn't ask to be taken to my favorite places,
the loft in the barn,
the banks of the Beaver,
the field where you can
see Black Mesa on a clear day.

She told me
she knew Daddy and I had a history before her,
and she wished she'd been there for the whole thing,
but she wasn't and there wasn't anything to do
but get over it and get on.

We both stared in wonder
at the pond my daddy made
and she said,
a hole like that says a lot about a man.

I didn't intend to, but I liked her,
because she was so plain and so honest,
and because she made Daddy laugh,
and me, too, just like that,
and even though I didn't know
if there was room for her
in me, I could see there was room for her in Daddy.
When I asked him if he wanted me
to go off to Aunt Ellis after all,
Daddy said he hadn't ever wanted it,
he said I was his own and he didn't like to
think about what Aunt Ellis might do with me.
And we laughed, picturing me and Aunt Ellis together,
and it wasn't a nice laugh, but it was
Aunt Ellis we were talking about after all.

---

2 **loft** top part of a barn where hay, etc., is kept – 15 **to intend** to want – 16 **plain** simple

The thing about Louise,
I'll just have to watch how things go and hope
she doesn't crowd me out of Daddy's life, not now,
when I am just finding my way back into it.

5   *October 1935*

Not Everywhere

I walk with Daddy
up the slope and look out over the Beaver River.
Louise is back at the house.
10 She wanted to come
but this is Ma's place,
Ma's grave,
Franklin's too,
and Louise has no business here.
15 She wants to come everywhere with us.
Well, I won't let her.
Not everywhere.

Daddy says,
"She could have come.
20 There's room enough for everyone, Billie Jo."
But there's not.
She can come into Ma's kitchen.
She can hang around the barn.
She can sit beside Daddy when he drives the truck.
25 But Ma's bones are in this hill,
Ma's and Franklin's.
And their bones wouldn't like it,
if Louise came walking up here between us.

October 1935

---

8 **slope** hill – 14 **to have no business here** to have no right to be here

142

My Life, or What I Told Louise
After the Tenth Time She Came to Dinner

"I may look like Daddy, but I have my mother's hands.
Piano hands, Ma called them,
sneaking a look at them any chance she got.
A piano is a grand thing," I say
"Though ours is covered in dust now.
Under the grime it's dark brown,
like my mother's eyes."

I think about the piano
and how above it hangs a mirror
and to either side of that mirror,
shelves,
where Ma and Daddy's wedding picture once stood,
though Daddy has taken that down.

"Whenever she could,
Ma filled a bowl with apples," I tell Louise.
"I'm crazy about apples,
and she filled a jar with wildflowers when she
found them,
and put them on that shelf above the piano."

On the other shelf Ma's book of poetry remains.
And the invitation from Aunt Ellis,
or what's left of it.
Daddy and I tore it into strips
to mark the poems we thought Ma liked best.

"We weren't always happy," I tell Louise.
"But we were happy enough
until the accident.

---

5 **to sneak a look at** to look at secretly – 18 **to be crazy about s.th.** to like s.th.
very much

When I rode the train west,
I went looking for something,
but I didn't see anything wonderful.
I didn't see anything better than what I already had.
5   Home."

I look straight into Louise's face.
Louise doesn't flinch.
She looks straight back.
I am the first one to back down.

10   "My hands don't look real pretty anymore.
But they hardly hurt. They only ache a little,
sometimes.
I could play right now,
maybe,
15   if I could get the dust out of the piano,
if I wanted to get the dust out of the piano.
But I don't. I'm not ready yet."

And what I like best about her,
is Louise doesn't say what I should do.
20   She just nods.
And I know she's heard everything I said,
and some things I didn't say too.

November 1935

November Dust

25   The wheat is growing
even though dust
blows in sometimes.

---

7 **to flinch** to move one's eyes, to look away – 9 **to back down** to give up, to
show that one is defeated

144

I walk with Daddy around the farm
and see that
the pond is holding its own,
it will keep Ma's apple trees alive,
nourish her garden,
help the grass around it grow,
enough to lie in and dream
if I feel like it,
and stand in,
and wait for Mad Dog
when he comes past once a week
on his way from Amarillo,
where he works for the radio.

And as long as the
dust doesn't crush
the winter wheat,
we'll have something to show in the spring
for all Daddy's hard work.
Not a lot, but more than last year.

November 1935

Thanksgiving List

Prairie birds, the whistle of gophers, the wind
blowing,
the smell of grass
and spicy earth,
friends like Mad Dog, the cattle down in the river,

---

3 **to hold one's own** *sich gut halten* – 5 **to nourish** ['nʌrɪʃ] to feed – 15 **to crush** to destroy – 17 **to have s.th. to show for** to have s.th. to present to the others – 21 **Thanksgiving** celebrated in the U.S. on the fourth Thursday in November – 22 **gopher** ground squirrel – 25 **spicy** full of spices *(gewürzt)*

water washing over their hooves,
the sky so
big, so full of
shifting clouds,
5   the cloud shadows creeping
over the fields,
Daddy's smile,
and his laugh,
and his songs,
10 Louise,
food without dust,
Daddy seeing to Ma's piano,
newly cleaned and tuned,
the days when my hands don't hurt at all,
15 the thank-you note from Lucille in Moline, Kansas,
the sound of rain,
Daddy's hole staying full of water
as the windmill turns,
the smell of green,
20 of damp earth,
of hope returning to our farm.
The poppies set to
bloom on Ma and Franklin's grave,
the morning with the whole day waiting,
25 full of promise,
the night
of quiet, of no expectations, of rest.
And the certainty of home, the one I live in,
and the one
30 that lives in me.

November 1935

---

4 **to shift** to change direction – 12 **to see to s.th.** to take care of s.th.

Music

I'm getting to know the music again.
And it is getting to know me.
We sniff each other's armpits,
and inside each other's ears,
and behind each other's necks.
We are both confident, and a little sassy.

And I know now that all the time I was trying to get
out of the dust,
the fact is,
what I am,
I am because of the dust.
And what I am is good enough.
Even for me.

November 1935

Teamwork

Louise and I take walks after dinne
every time she comes.
By the time we get back
the kitchen looks pretty good,
Daddy only leaves a few things he doesn't
understand,
like big pans,
and wooden spoons,
and leftovers,
and that makes me a little irritated
but mostly it makes me love him.

---

4 **to sniff** to smell – **armpit** place under the arm – 7 **sassy** rude – 26 **irritated** angry

And Louise, knowing exactly what's left to be done,
helps me finish up.

She was my father's teacher at the night school class.
She never married.
5   She went to college for two years
and studied and worked,
and didn't notice how lonely she was
until she met Daddy and fell into the
big hurt of his eyes.
10   She knows how to keep a home,
she knows how to cook,
she knows how to make things
last through winters
and drought.

15   She knows how to smooth things between two
redheaded people.
And she knows how to come into a home
and not step on the toes of a ghost.
I still feel grateful she didn't make cranberry sauce
20   last month, at the first Thanksgiving we
spent together.
Louise made sweet potatoes and green beans,
and turkey, and two pies, pumpkin
and chocolate.
25   I was so full
my lids
sighed shut and Daddy walked with Louise instead of me
out to Ma and Franklin's grave,
where he let Ma know his intentions.
30   And Ma's bones didn't object.
Neither did mine.

---

9 **hurt** pain – 26 **lid** eyelid – 30 **to object** to mind, to have s.th. against

And when they came back to the house,
Daddy still cleaned the kitchen.

December 1935

Finding a Way

Daddy
started talking
about planting
the rest of the acres in wheat,
but then said, No,
let's just go with what we've got right now.

And I've
been playing
a half hour
every day,
making the skin stretch,
making the scars stretch.

The way I see it, hard times aren't only
about money,
or drought,
or dust.
Hard times are about losing spirit,
and hope,
and what happens when dreams dry up.

The tractor's busted,
we don't have the cash to fix it,
but there's nothing saying Daddy can't do the work
by hand.

---

21 **to lose spirit** to lose hope – 24 **busted** broken – 25 **to fix** *here:* to repair

It can't be any harder than digging a hole
forty by sixty by six feet deep.

Daddy bought a second mule with Louise's help.
Her betrothal gift to him.
5   He walks behind the team,
step by step, listing the fields to fight the wind.
Maybe the tractor lifted him above the land,
maybe the fields didn't know him anymore,
didn't remember the touch of his feet,
10 or the stroke of his hand,
or the bones of his knees,
and why should wheat grow for a stranger?
Daddy said he'd try some sorghum,
maybe some cotton,
15 admitting as how there might be something
to this notion of diversification folks were
talking about,
and yes, he'd bring the grass back
like Ma wanted,
20 where he wasn't planting anything else.
He'd make new sod.
And I'm learning, watching Daddy, that you can stay
in one place
and still grow.

25 I wipe dust out of the roasting pan,
I wipe dust off Ma's dishes,
and wait for Daddy to drive in with Louise,
hoping she'll stay a little later,
a little longer,
30 waiting for the day when she stays for good.

---

4 **betrothal** [bɪ'trəʊðəl] wedding – 5 **team** *here:* two animals hitched together to
do a job – 6 **to list** to protect the edge of a field by a small furrow – 16 **notion
of diversification** idea that different plants and crops are better for the land –
25 **roasting pan** pan for making roasts *(Bratpfanne)* – 30 **for good** forever

She wears a comical hat, with flowers,
in December,
and when she smiles,
her face is
full enough of springtime, it makes
her hat seem just right.
She brings apples in a sack,
perfect apples she arranges
in a bowl on the shelf,
opposite the book of poetry.
Sometimes, while I'm at the piano,
I catch her reflection in the mirror,
standing in the kitchen, soft-eyed, while Daddy
finishes chores,
and I stretch my fingers over the keys,
and I play.

December 1935

Supplementary Texts

1. Mean Clouds

The following text is an excerpt from Children of the Dust Bowl, *which tells the story of the "Okie" migration to California and of the school at Weedpatch Camp, where migrant children*
5 *found a temporary home.*

Life had always been hard on the farmers who lived in Oklahoma, and in the 1930s it was especially hard on those who lived in the Panhandle, a barren stretch of rock and red soil sandwiched between Texas, Kansas and New Mexico. These people owned
10 small family farms of forty to eighty acres and were "dry farmers". They had no irrigation system, no reservoirs to store water, no canals to bring water to their farms. When there was enough rain, the Okies in the Panhandle grew wheat and corn and raised cattle. When there wasn't enough rain, they were forced to sell their
15 livestock and farm machinery and borrow money from the bank. Every year they gambled with their lives, hoping for enough rain to get by.

   In 1931 it stopped raining in the Panhandle. The sky became bright and hot, and it stayed that way every day. Cornstalks in the
20 fields shriveled from the sizzling heat. Shoots of wheat dried up

---

3 **Okie** nickname for a person from Oklahoma – **migration** [maɪˈɡreɪʃn] move from one place to another – 4 **migrant** [ˈmaɪɡrənt] moving from one place to another to escape hardship, etc. – 8 **Panhandle** part of Oklahoma (see map p. 155) – **barren** not or hardly producing plants – **soil** upper layer of the earth in which plants grow (*Boden*) – **sandwiched** pressed between two things – 10 **acre** 4047 square meters – 11 **irrigation** the supplying of water to dry land (*Bewässerung*) – **to store** to keep – 13 **wheat** a type of grain (*Weizen*) – **corn** a type of grain (*Mais*) – 14 **livestock** farm animals – 16 **to gamble** to take a risk, to bet (money) on – **to get by** to stay alive, to make a living – 18 **cornstalk** [stɔːk] main stem of a corn plant (*Halm*) – 19 **to shrivel** to dry up – **sizzling** very hot (*sengend*) – **shoot** young leaf or stem

and fell to the ground. The farmers were caught in an impossible situation. They were already suffering from the effects of the Great Depression, which had started in 1929 when the stock market collapsed. The Depression caused the price of wheat and corn to fall so low that it made growing these crops unprofitable. Most farmers had borrowed money to buy their land and had borrowed again against their land in lean years. When the prices for their crops fell, many couldn't make payments to the banks that held title to their land. By 1932 one thousand families a week in Texas, Oklahoma, and Arkansas were losing their farms to the banks. And now it had stopped raining in the Panhandle, and the crops themselves were failing.

Then when it seemed that things couldn't get any worse, they did. The year was 1936. It hadn't rained more than a few drops in the Panhandle for five straight years. One day the wind started to blow, and every day it blew harder and harder, as if nature were playing a cruel joke on the Okies. The wind blew the dry soil into the air, and every morning the sun rose only do disappear behind a sky of red dirt and dust. The wind knocked open doors, shattered windows, and leveled barns.

It became known as the great Dust Bowl, and it was centered in the Panhandle near Goodwell, Oklahoma.

From *Children of the Dust Bowl,* by Jerry Stanley, copyright © 1992 by Jerry Stanley, pp. 3-4. Used by permission of Crown Children's Books, a division of Random House, Inc.

---

2 **Great Depression** period of great economic problems, 1929 – 1939 –
3 **stock market** stock exchange *(Börse)* – 5 **crop** plant product grown by a farmer – 7 **lean** opposite of *fat; here:* difficult – 9 **to hold title to s.th.** to own –
20 **to level** to destroy, to throw down *(dem Erdboden gleich machen)* –
21 **Dust Bowl** area in Oklahoma, Texas, Colorado and Kansas affected by the dust storms

2. Mother Road – Route 66

The following is also an excerpt from Children of the Dust Bowl.

The advertisements for workers led to what is called the Dust Bowl migration. It was the largest migration of people in U.S. his-
5 tory. Between 1935 and 1940 over one million people left their homes in Oklahoma, Texas, Arkansas, and Missouri and moved to California. Most of the migrants were white, but the exodus from the southwestern states also included some black families. Among the migrants, 375,000 Okies cursed the wind, the dirt, and the
10 drought one last time, then set out for "Californ-I-A."

And what a sight it was! The Okies sold what few valuable possessions they still had: an old tractor, a plow, perhaps a cow that had survived. Then aunts and uncles, brothers and sisters, parents and grandparents, pooled their money to buy an old
15 jalopy, or a beat-up flatbed truck. Soon the vehicle would be loaded down with tools, pots, pans, bulging suitcases, guitars, washtubs, and mattresses. And always, straddling the ten-foot-high mountain of family possessions, there were children, often six or more, whose job it was to make sure the ropes stayed tight and
20 nothing was lost.

For others there was nothing to sell, nothing to pack. Many of these Okies "rode the rail" to California, sneaking aboard empty railroad boxcars heading west. [...]

Then one by one the overloaded trucks sputtered onto Route
25 66, which Okies called Mother Road. Today, most of old Route 66 is closed or in a state of disrepair. But the Okies who rode Mother

---

7 **exodus** ['eksədəs] mass emigration from one place – 9 **to curse** to damn, to wish that evil will befall s.o. or s.th. *(verfluchen)* – 10 **drought** [draʊt] period with no rain – **Californ-I-A** [ˌkælɪfɔːnaɪˈeɪ] – 11 **sight** spectacle *(Anblick)* – 14 **to pool** to put together, to combine – 15 **jalopy** [dʒəˈlɒpɪ] *(informal)* an old run-down car – **flatbed truck** truck with an open loading area with no sides *(Pritschenwagen)* – 16 **bulging** so full they are round – 17 **straddling** *here:* on top – 19 **to make sure** to watch – **tight** not loose – 22 **to sneak aboard** to get secretly on – 24 **to sputter** to make hissing and popping sounds – 26 **disrepair** poor condition

Road to California will never forget the blast-furnace heat, the winding mountain roads, the bridgeless rocky paths, the washed-out mud banks, the hunger, and the uncertainty that threatened them every mile of the way. When Okies recall the Dust Bowl migration, they remember every town: first Shamrock and Amarillo in northern Texas, then Tucumcari and Albuquerque in New Mexico; on to Holbrook, Flagstaff, and Kingman in Arizona, and then Needles and Barstow as they entered California. They remember every hardship and every happy moment.

From *Children of the Dust Bowl*, by Jerry Stanley, copyright © 1992 by Jerry Stanley, pp. 12-15. Used by permission of Crown Children's Books, a division of Random House, Inc.

---

1 **blast-furnace** ['fɜːnɪs] place in which iron is smelted *(Hochofen)* – 2 **to wind** [waɪnd] – 4 **to recall** to remember

3. Map of Oklahoma and Northern Texas

From the Scholastic Literature Guide for *Out of the Dust*, written by Linda Ward Beech. Copyright © 2000 by Scholastic, Inc. Used by permission.

4. Dusty Old Dust (Woody Guthrie)

This song is one of Woody Guthrie's Dust Bowl Ballads, *which were recorded in 1940. Woody Guthrie, a native of Oklahoma, was born in 1912 and died in 1967.*

5   I've sung this song, but I'll sing it again,
Of the place that I lived on the wild windy plains,
In the month called April, county called Gray,
And here's what all of the people there say:

CHORUS:
10 "So long, it's been good to know yuh;
So long, it's been good to know yuh;
So long, it's been good to know yuh.
This dusty old dust is a-gettin' my home,
And I got to be driftin' along."

15 A dust storm hit, an' it hit like thunder;
It dusted us over, an' it covered us under;
Blocked out the traffic an' blocked out the sun,
Straight for home all the people did run,
Singin':
20 CHORUS

We talked of the end of the world, and then
We'd sing a song an' then sing it again.
We'd sit for an hour an' not say a word,
And then these words would be heard:
25 CHORUS

---

7 **Gray** county in the Texas Panhandle, east of Amarillo – 10 **yuh** [jə] you – 14 **to drift along** to move on – 15 **thunder** loud noise to be heard after lightning *(Donner)*

Sweethearts sat in the dark and sparked,
They hugged and kissed in that dusty old dark.
They sighed and cried, hugged and kissed,
Instead of marriage, they talked like this:
"Honey..."
CHORUS

Now, the telephone rang, an' it jumped off the wall,
That was the preacher, a-makin' his call.
He said, "Kind friend, this may the end;
An' you got your last chance of salvation of sin!"
CHORUS

The churches was jammed, and the churches was packed,
An' that dusty old dust storm blowed so black.
Preacher could not read a word of his text,
An' he folded his specs, an' he took up collection,
Said:
CHORUS

Text Woody Guthrie (tune "Ballad of Billie the Kid" & "Goodnight, Irene" 1935) © Essex Musikvertrieb, Hamburg

---

26 **to spark** *(AE informal)* to flirt, to try to win the favor of a woman or man one loves – 28 **to sigh** to utter a low tone of worry *(seufzen)* – 35 **salvation of sin** *here: Vergebung der Sünden* – 37 **jammed** very full – **packed** crowded – 38 **blowed** blew – 40 **specs** *(informal)* spectacles, glasses

5. An Excerpt from *The Grapes of Wrath* by John Steinbeck

In 1939 John Steinbeck (1902–1968) published his novel The
Grapes of Wrath, *which deals with the fate of the Joad family,
who left Oklahoma for California to escape the Dust Bowl. The*
5 *narrative chapters of the novel alternate with chapters dealing
with the social significance of the events. The excerpt below is
from Chapter 21 of the novel.*

In the West there was panic when the migrants multiplied on the
highways. Men of property were terrified for their property. Men
10 who had never been hungry saw the eyes of the hungry. Men who
had never wanted anything very much saw the flare of want in the
eyes of the migrants. And the men of the towns and of the soft
suburban country gathered to defend themselves; and they
reassured themselves that they were good and the invaders bad, as
15 a man must do before he fights. They said, These goddamned
Okies are dirty and ignorant. They're degenerate, sexual maniacs.
These goddamned Okies are thieves. They'll steal anything.
They've got no sense of property rights.

And the latter was true, for how can a man without property
20 know the ache of ownership? And the defending people said,
They bring disease, they're filthy. We can't have them in the
schools. They're strangers. How'd you like to have your sister go
out with one of 'em?

The local people whipped themselves into a mold of cruelty.
25 Then they formed units, squads, and armed them – armed them

---

5 **to alternate** to happen in turns *(sich abwechseln)* – 6 **significance** importance,
meaning – 8 **migrant** ['maɪɡrənt] person moving from place to place looking for
work – 9 **men of property** owners of land, houses, etc. – **terrified** frightened –
11 **flare** outbreak, expression – **want** need, poverty; s.th. desired – 13 **to gather**
to come together – **to reassure** [ˌriːəˈʃɔː] to calm, to comfort – 14 **invader** person
who enters by force *(Eindringling)* – 16 **degenerate** [dɪˈdʒenərət] decadent,
without moral standards – **sexual maniac** person who is fixated on sex – 19 **the
latter** the last thing mentioned – 20 **ache** [eɪk] steady pain – 21 **filthy** very dirty
– 24 **mold** (BE mould) *here:* form, shape, attitude – 25 **squad** [skwɒd] a group
of people organized for a special purpose – **to arm s.o.** to give s.o. weapons

with clubs, with gas, with guns. We own the country. We can't let these Okies get out of hand. And the men who were armed did not own the land, but they thought they did. And the clerks who drilled at night owned nothing, and the little storekeepers possessed only a drawerful of debts. But even a debt is something, even a job is something. The clerk thought, I get fifteen dollars a week. S'pose a goddamn Okie would work for twelve? And the little storekeeper thought, How could I compete with a debtless man?

And the migrants streamed in on the highways and their hunger was in their eyes, and their need was in their eyes. They had no argument, no system, nothing but their numbers and their needs. When there was work for a man, ten men fought for it – fought with a low wage. If that fella'll work for thirty cents, I'll work for twenty-five.

If he'll take twenty-five, I'll do it for twenty.

No, me, I'm hungry. I'll work for fifteen. I'll work for food. The kids. You ought to see them. Little boils, like, comin' out, an' they can't run aroun'. Give 'em some windfall fruit, an' they bloated up. Me. I'll work for a little piece of meat.

And this was good, for wages went down and prices stayed up. The great owners were glad and they sent out more handbills to bring more people in. And wages went down and prices stayed up. And pretty soon now we'll have serfs again.

"Chapter 21", from *The Grapes of Wrath* by John Steinbeck, copyright 1939, renewed © 1967 by John Steinbeck. Used by permission of Viking Penguin, a division of Penguin Putnam Inc.

---

1 **club** heavy piece of wood used for hitting – 3 **clerk** *(AE)* employee who works in a shop, shop assistant – 4 **to drill** to do military exercises – 5 **to possess** to own – **drawerful** a drawer *(= Schublade)* full of – **debt** [det] money one owes to s.o. *(Schulden)* – 7 **s'pose** suppose, imagine – 8 **to compete** to try to win – 14 **wage(s)** money one gets for one's work – **fella** fellow, man – 18 **boils** a painful swelling of the skin *(Geschwür)* – 19 **bloated up** swollen – 22 **handbill** leaflet – 24 **serf** slave